Club Wicked 1:
MY WICKED VALENTINE

Ann Mayburn

LooseId.

ISBN 13: 978-1-62300-629-7
CLUB WICKED 1: MY WICKED VALENTINE
Copyright © November 2013 by Ann Mayburn
Originally released in e-book format in February 2013

Cover Art by Fiona Jayde
Cover Layout and Design by April Martinez

All rights reserved. Except for use of brief quotations in any review or critical article, the reproduction or utilization of this work in whole or in part in any form by any electronic, mechanical or other means, now known or hereafter invented, including xerography, photo-copying and recording, or in any information storage or retrieval is forbidden without the prior written permission of Loose Id LLC, PO Box 809, San Francisco CA 94104-0809. http://www.loose-id.com

Image/art disclaimer: Licensed material is being used for illustrative purposes only. Any person depicted in the licensed material is a model.

DISCLAIMER: Many of the acts described in our BDSM/fetish titles can be dangerous. Please do not try any new sexual practice, whether it be fire, rope, or whip play, without the guidance of an experienced practitioner. Neither Loose Id nor its authors will be responsible for any loss, harm, injury or death resulting from use of the information contained in any of its titles.

This book is an original publication of Loose Id. Each individual story herein was previously published in e-book format only by Loose Id and is a work of fiction. Any similarity to actual persons, events or existing locations is entirely coincidental.

Printed in the U.S.A. by
Lightning Source, Inc.
1246 Heil Quaker Blvd
La Vergne TN 37086
www.lightningsource.com

Dedication

*A flower cannot bloom without sunshine,
and a man cannot live without love.*
—Max Muller

Acknowledgment

To my beloved readers, it is for you that I created this world, so that in it, you can lose yourself in the arms of a man worthy of the priceless gift of your submission.

To my fabulous beta-fish goddesses: Annette Stone, Dawn, Cari Quinn, Catharine J., Kerry Vail, and Dawn Marie. You have my eternal thanks for helping me bring Wicked to life. ☺

Chapter One

Lucia Roa jabbed the illuminated button for the twelfth floor with a shaking finger. As the doors slowly slid shut, she tried to take in a calming breath but only succeeded in gasping for air like a drowning swimmer. The floor beneath her cute royal-blue heels shifted as the elevator began its upward climb, and her heartbeat increased with every floor.

Why had she let her mentor, Mrs. Florentine, talk her into this? At the time it had seemed like a great idea. Mrs. Florentine had an inside scoop on one of Washington, DC's private and influential clubs needing a new party planner, and she just knew Lucia would be perfect for the job. Of course Lucia had never planned a party for anything bigger than a two-hundred person bar mitzvah, and she had only recently graduated with an associate's degree from the local community college.

She was also the daughter of Mexican immigrants and still worked twenty hours a week at her family's restaurant to make ends meet—which was a blessing because last month she'd had to choose between groceries and having her lights on—but sure she was totally the best pick for throwing a party for some of the most influential people in DC. Oh, and Mrs. Florentine wouldn't say what kind of private club this was or what kinds of parties they expected.

Lucia was so going to nail this job.

Sure.

"*Dress sexy,*" Mrs. Florentine had said. "*Wear some-*

thing that shows off your lovely curves. Own your femininity." So now not only was she going into a business meeting woefully unprepared, she also felt like a tart. Instead of the usual classy gray suit she wore to meetings, she was dressed in a tight-fitting white pencil skirt that more than showed off her ample curves. She paired the skirt with a royal-blue jacket that flattered her caramel-colored skin while hiding her overdeveloped chest. The last thing she wanted was to spend a business meeting with a man staring at her boobs instead of her face. The men riding the Metro with her that morning had certainly appreciated her outfit, if the catcalls and suggestive comments meant anything.

The elevator binged as it reached her floor, and she almost dropped her briefcase. The doors slid open to reveal an elegant reception room brightly lit by the sunlight streaming in the big windows. A white circular receptionist's desk dominated the center of the room, and the impeccably dressed receptionist gave her a warm smile as she stepped out of the elevator. Two other women sat in the white leather chairs flanking the desk, and they both turned to face her.

The receptionist spoke into the phone at her desk before looking over at Lucia. "Welcome to O'Keefe Industries. How may I help you?"

Lucia plastered what she hoped was a pleasant smile on her face and walked past the two waiting women to the desk. "Hello. My name is Lucia Roa, and I have an appointment with Mr. O'Keefe."

The receptionist looked down at her computer screen and nodded. "You're a tad early, and Mr. O'Keefe is running a bit late. Please have a seat. Can I get you anything to drink while you wait?"

"No, I'm fine, thank you." While she would have loved some coffee, she could just see herself spilling it all over her clothes.

She took a seat across from the other two women, conscious of how closely they watched her. Lucia recognized the woman on the left, a lovely and perky blonde in a cream suit, from the society pages of the newspaper and the local magazines. Her heart sank as she stole a glance at the woman on the right. Mary Wellington, descendant of the Wellington oil family and prominent fixture in Washington, DC, society. Also one of the premier party planners with more connections than Lucia could ever dream of having.

She almost slumped back into her chair but caught herself. No, she wasn't going to give up before she even met with Mr. O'Keefe. So maybe she had as much of a chance at landing this job as she had of being recruited for the Tijuana soccer team, but darn it, with the right resources, she could throw as good of a party as any of these women. After all, her family's Tex-Mex restaurant catered many of the top events in Washington, and she'd probably been to more corporate balls and gatherings than both women combined. True, she'd attended them as a waitress, but she paid attention to the small details.

The perky blonde got called in next, and Lucia crossed her legs, resisting the urge to dig through her briefcase and double-check her proposal. Well, actually *proposals*. She really had no idea what kind of event they needed a planner for, but she had proposals for everything from a ball to a polo match to a wine tasting.

Mary Wellington looked down her patrician nose and said in a nasally voice, "Pardon me, you look familiar. Have we met before?"

Lucia flushed and shrank back into her seat. They'd run into each other dozens of times over the years, but always while Lucia was working for her family's restaurant and catering business as a waitress. "I'm not sure. You seem familiar too."

Mary tapped her lips with a pale pink manicured nail. "Oh, I know what it is." She gave Lucia a smile that would have looked right at home on a shark. "You're one of the Roa girls. Are you here for the catering position?"

Lucia gave an equally insincere smile. "No, I'm here for the event planner job."

The corners of Mary's thin lips turned up. "Really?"

"Yes." The word came out in a soft whisper, and Lucia cleared her throat. "I recently started my own event planning company."

"How...charming."

Clutching her briefcase on her lap with both hands, Lucia barely resisted the urge to smack that smug smile off the other woman's face. "Thank you."

Mary opened her mouth to say something else, but the perky blonde stormed through the reception area. She paused and gave both of them a heated look. "Good luck dealing with that asshole." She turned on her heel and marched to the waiting elevator.

Both Mary and Lucia gaped at the blonde's back as she stalked into the elevator's cab while the receptionist shook her head. The phone on her desk rang, and she picked it up with a forced smile. "Ms. Roa, he's ready for you. His office is at the end of the hall."

Lucia ignored Mary's sniff of disdain as she stood and smoothed her tight skirt. "Thank you."

She went down the quiet hallway, passing beautiful works of art hanging on the walls next to brass name plates on closed office doors. Her heels sank into the thick cream carpeting, and she paused before the door at the end of the hall, wiping her sweaty palms on her jacket. The brass plate next to this door simply read Isaac O'Keefe, CEO.

Okay, this was it, the meeting that would either put her event planning company on the map or be another waste of Metro fare. She knocked on the door and opened it after a muffled "The door's open" came from the other side.

All the breath left her body in a soft whoosh as the most handsome man she'd ever seen sat at his desk. She had a brief impression of a large, well-lit corner office with a view of the Capitol, but all she could really focus on was him. A lock of his thick black hair fell over his forehead, and she had the inane urge to brush it away. He didn't look up as she entered or say anything, so she paused in the doorway, unsure of what to do. A slight shadow of scruff darkened his square jaw.

Then he glanced up, and her world became suffused with burning cold. Ice-blue eyes, so pale they were almost white, stared at her. She felt stripped to the bottom of her soul. Heat immersed her, and when he licked his lower lip, her nipples puckered to stiff peaks beneath her suit jacket, and she was afraid she might spontaneously combust from desire.

She was in so much trouble.

Isaac leaned back in his chair and tried to keep his lust under control. An unusually beautiful woman stood in the doorway, framed by a ray of sunlight. She wasn't perfect, like the stunning and plastic society women he was used to, but there was something about her that called to him. She was all softness, heat, and if the warm look she was giving him was any indication, his attraction wasn't one-sided.

Her expression turned questioning, and he realized she was waiting to be invited into his office. He brushed his hair off his forehead and smiled. "Welcome, Ms. Roa. Please have a seat."

When she turned to shut the door behind her, his cock twitched in interest. He'd always been an ass man. She had an amazingly round ass, high and tight. The kind of ass he could grab with both hands. The kind of ass that would cushion the hard fucking he wanted to give her while she was tied to his bedpost.

Whoa, where did those thoughts come from?

What the hell was wrong with him? This was a potential employee, not a delicious woman he'd love to do wicked things with. He mentally tried to shut the door on his libido, but when she crossed the room, she reminded him of the way a cat walked, all sensual grace. He wondered if she was new in town, because he surely would have remembered a submissive like this at the club.

They shook hands, and she sat down across from him. After she cleared her throat, she looked around for where to place her briefcase. Young, not more than twenty-five, but with soft baby cheeks that made her seem younger. Her dark brown eyes had a slight tilt to them, and she had that lovely golden-brown skin color he adored on women. When his gaze reached her lips, he shifted at how full they looked beneath her light coating of lip gloss. The things he could do to those lips.

Her shoulders tensed, and he returned his attention to her eyes. A bit of fire sparked there; that intrigued him even more. The smooth roll of her lightly accented voice washed over him. "Nice to meet you, Mr. O'Keefe. I'm here about the Valentine's Day party."

"A pleasure to meet you, Ms. Roa."

She reached into her briefcase and pulled out an elegant black portfolio and placed it on his desk. "Thank you for meeting with me."

He picked up her folder and looked through it, buying himself some time to gather his wits. Her list of past experience was good, but it mostly consisted of children's parties. He didn't expect her to have her more adult parties listed in her portfolio and appreciated her discretion, but he couldn't judge her ability to throw a party for Club Wicked on how many bar mitzvahs she'd planned.

"Ms. Roa, do you have any experience with adult parties?"

She flushed, and her gaze darted over his shoulder. "Not a great deal, but I assure you the events I have orchestrated have all been well received." She gestured toward the portfolio. "If you look in the back, you will see my list of references."

Confused, he flipped to the last page and scanned it. How did she hear about the job if she had no experience in the field? He scanned the last few pages, hoping for some indication as to how she'd ended up on the other side of his desk. The event planner position hadn't been listed on any public sources, so someone must have told her about it. A list of glowing accolades from her past clients made up the end part of her portfolio. On the last page was a letter of recommendation from Mrs. Sara Florentine.

Shit.

He groaned and closed the portfolio. "I'm sorry, but I have to make a quick call. I think you've been sent here by mistake."

Hurt flashed through her eyes, but she stood and started to reach for the portfolio. "I see, but if you would just look—"

He placed his hand over it and shook his head. "I'm not asking you to leave. I just want to talk to Mrs. Florentine. She's a personal friend of mine."

Lucia's relief was palpable as she sank back into her chair with a smile. "Oh, well, of course."

He took his cell phone from his pocket and scrolled through his list of contacts, finding one Mrs. Florentine, who had a great deal to answer for. What was that woman thinking, sending an innocent young thing like that to him for the Valentine's Day event? If Ms. Roa even knew what kind of club Wicked was, he'd eat his tie.

The phone rang once, and then the voice of the chairman of the board's wife and co-owner of Wicked came over the line. "Isaac! What a pleasure to hear from you."

He turned to the side and replied in Sara's native French to keep their conversation private. "What are you up to?"

"Why, whatever do you mean?" The amusement in her tone was evident, and it raised his hackles. Sara viewed herself as Wicked's resident matchmaker and seemed to be particularly offended by his adamant refusal to settle down.

He thought she'd given up on finding him anyone to fit his rather prickly personality, but evidently she'd been biding her time. He glanced over at Lucia, who was gazing out the window, obviously trying to give him some semblance of privacy. "You know exactly what I mean. What are you doing sending this innocent to me for the Valentine's Day party? I need a person who is familiar with our lifestyle, not someone who has a clown that makes balloon animals on speed dial."

"Oh, pishposh. She is extremely intelligent, very hardworking, and has a brilliant imagination. I mentored her myself as part of my work through the college. If you don't hire her, you are being a complete idiot. Besides, you could always mentor her and teach her everything she needs to know about Wicked and the dark pleasures we offer."

That thought was very appealing, but he pushed it away and tried to focus on reality. "This isn't a Sweet Sixteen party, Sara. This is a very adult function—"

Lucia's husky voice interrupted him. "Actually, the Sweet Sixteen party was more for the mother than the teenager, so that could count as an adult party."

After all he'd seen, all he'd done, he rarely felt

embarrassed anymore, but sure enough that old feeling came flooding back. "Sara, I have to go." He hung up on the sound of her laughing and rubbed his face before facing a rather irate Lucia. "Forgive me. I didn't realize you spoke French."

"I took it in high school and college." She gave him a level look. "So I understood you believe I'm too innocent to help you throw a successful party?"

"I'm sorry. You don't quite understand what is going on here, and I really don't think you're the right person for this job."

She stood, but instead of leaving, she placed both of her hands on his desk and leaned over, the sheaf of her dark hair falling over her shoulder in a tempting tangle of curls. "Look, I may be young, but I'm far from innocent. Whatever kind of party you need, I can do it, and I can do it better than anyone else you've seen today."

He found her ire adorable, though he was pretty sure he didn't want to see her really angry. Exasperated at trying to tiptoe around it, he decided to tell her the truth. "In all honesty, Ms. Roa, this Valentine's Day party is for a private and very exclusive BDSM club. Something I'm pretty sure you have no clue about."

"That doesn't mean I can't do a party! I'm a very quick learner, and I always research the background needs for whoever my client is. So I don't know what BDSM is. I can learn."

The thought of her bound, bent over a spanking bench, ready to be fucked filled his mind. Clearing his throat, he sat forward, hoping she couldn't see how hard she'd made him. He bit the inside of his cheek to keep from laughing at how cute she looked when she was pissed. So much fire in her gaze.

"It stands for Bondage, Discipline, Sadism, and Masochism."

"What?" She closed her eyes and took a deep breath. "Like whips and chains and stuff?"

"Not really, but for the purpose of this discussion, yes."

Her jaw dropped, and she sat back in her chair. "Are you for real?"

He covered his eyes and fought to keep from laughing. Here she was, his walking wet dream, and she couldn't be more wrong for him. "Yes, we are very for real."

The silence stretched out between them. When he looked up, he found her studying him. "I can still do your party."

"Ms. Roa, you have to be reasonable. You can't fake knowing what the lifestyle is like. I'll be honest with you. I have a great deal riding on the success of the Valentine's Day bash. If I do a good job, my place on the board of directors at Wicked is pretty much guaranteed. I want that spot. I need this party to be a success, and while I truly do admire what you've done with your company in the year you've been open, I really need someone familiar with the lifestyle."

"What's Wicked?"

He couldn't help but feel a little bit of pride as he said, "Wicked was founded in 1916 and is the oldest and most influential BDSM club in DC. We've had everyone from presidents to movie stars as members."

She blinked rapidly as she digested that information. "I still say I can do it if you would just give me a chance. Anything you want, I can do, and if I can't do it, I can find someone who will."

Frustrated at her stubbornness, turned on by her insistence that she could do what he wanted while being plagued by what he wanted to do to her, he tried to get himself under control. He folded his hands on the desk and decided to be a little more direct. "Reading books and watching videos will not help you truly understand how Wicked and its members think and react. You have to understand the mind of a submissive and Dominant, to immerse yourself in the lifestyle." He took a deep breath and blew it out, trying to banish the thought of her kneeling before him, her head tipped back, and her eyes closed as she awaited his command or his touch. "Ms. Roa, I need an event planner who can work with me, more as a partnership than anything else. The only way I could do that with you is to introduce you to the world of BDSM as my submissive."

She gave him a suspicious glare and crossed her arms over her chest. "What does that mean?"

"It means I would be responsible for you in the club. I would also be in charge of educating you on BDSM. I would also, temporarily, be your Master." As soon as he said those words, he realized he really did want to be her Master, however briefly. The thought of being the first to introduce her to his world made everything in his body catch fire. More than that, the idea of her wearing his collar seemed right.

Her big brown eyes grew wide, and her breath came out in a gasp before she said, "Oh hell no!" She stood and stuffed her portfolio into her briefcase. "I am not going to sleep with you for a job."

"I never said that." He tried to keep his voice under control, but some of his anger seeped through. "I would never, ever force a woman to have sex with me in exchange for a job. I'm rather insulted that you would think that."

She stood and clutched her briefcase with both hands. "You said you want to be my Master. To me that sounds like some kind of kinky sex thing."

He sighed and rubbed his face. Normally he could sweet-talk a woman into anything he wanted, but it looked like Lucia was going to be a hard sell. Oddly enough that thought aroused him, the additional edge of wanting something he couldn't have. There wasn't a man alive who didn't like a bit of a chase. "Look, when you get home, call Mrs. Florentine. Talk to her and let her know I offered to mentor you as your Master and what *you* think that means."

A dark pink blush stained her cheeks. "I most certainly will not talk about my sex life with Mrs. Florentine!"

The more she protested, the more he wanted to show her how wrong she was about not wanting anything to do with BDSM. She had no idea of the pleasure he could give her. "Do you really want to throw away an opportunity like this because of your fear of the unknown?"

She clenched her jaw, and her lips tightened. "I'm not afraid. You're creeping me out."

He stared at her in disbelief. No woman had ever found him creepy before. Ever. Her opinion actually hurt his ego, something he didn't think was possible. Good God, when had he become so jaded that he misread a woman this badly? More importantly, why did he care what this woman who'd known him for less than twenty minutes thought of him? He didn't give a flying fuck what anyone thought; that was one of the things that defined his life. But it did matter what she thought of him, and he found himself defending his character yet again.

"Ms. Roa, let me assure you if I'm ever in need of female company, I have never lacked a partner."

That made her pause. "Then why don't you call one of them for a good time?"

The urge to laugh stuck in his throat, and he swallowed hard. He had a feeling that laughing at Ms. Roa would be the wrong thing to do. "Because they don't have your talent for design. Your portfolio shows me you have a new, fresh vision for entertaining, and I like it. The last woman who came in wanted to do cakes shaped like giant penises that would spray frosting out of the tip."

Her lips quirked. "That is rather tacky."

"Indeed. More importantly, I believe the members would like whatever we come up with. I wasn't lying when I said I admire what you've done. You have good taste, and that is something money can't buy." He didn't add that Mrs. Florentine would be offended by his inability to get along with a woman she was obviously attempting to set him up with. "Please, give it some thought. I'll keep the position open until Monday. If you change your mind, please give me a call."

She hesitated, then squared her shoulders and lifted her chin. "I'm not promising anything."

"I know, but I'm asking you to at least consider the position. Remember, I'm offering you a partnership with equal say on the planning."

She snorted and cocked her hip. "That's not all you're offering me."

"No, it isn't, but do you really think Mrs. Florentine went to the efforts of securing you an interview with me only to get me laid?" He pulled out his wallet and handed her his personal card. "Here. This has my cell number and e-mail on it. If you have any questions, please don't hesitate to contact me."

She took the card from him, and he made sure not to touch her even though he would love to see if her skin was as soft as it looked.

"I'll call Mrs. Florentine and talk with her, but that's it."

"Thank you, Ms. Roa."

He stood to walk her to the door, but she quickly moved across the room and opened it herself as if she were afraid he'd pounce on her. "Have a good day, Mr. O'Keefe."

Before he could respond, she shut the door and left him staring at the wooden surface with a mixture of emotions swirling through his mind. Amusement filled him that she obviously thought he was some type of pervert. No, what did she call him? Oh yes, a creep. After having submissives literally throwing themselves at his feet, it was refreshing, if a bit disconcerting, to find a woman who didn't instantly give in to his every wish.

He chuckled and sat back down at his desk, humming as he sent an e-mail to his security staff to make sure Ms. Roa would pass a background check. With the high-level CEOs and political dignitaries who frequented Wicked, they could never be too careful about who they let into their club. The checks took a bit of time, and he wanted the paperwork pushed through as quickly as possible for when Ms. Roa agreed to his terms.

And there wasn't a doubt she would agree, eventually—at least he hoped she would.

He worked hard for everything he had and would do everything he could to sway her decision in his favor. What he'd told her had been true; he saw a great deal of potential in her work, but more than that she intrigued him. Being born into and raised around immense amounts of money, he was used to women trying to make themselves into what they thought he wanted. With Ms. Roa, he didn't think that was going to be a problem. She obviously had no problem telling him exactly what she thought, and he had a feeling she didn't take shit from anyone. Hell, she'd put him in his place without batting a lash once she felt he'd insulted her. It was refreshing to have someone speak their mind instead of automatically saying whatever they thought he wanted to hear. The world was filled with ass kissers, but honest people were rare.

Too bad he could only introduce her to the world of BDSM and not keep her as his own submissive. That thought made him pause. No, he didn't want a commitment like that. He'd promised himself years ago he would never fall in love again, and so far he'd managed to keep that promise. He was happy with his bachelor lifestyle and didn't want to change it.

An image of Ms. Roa—Lucia—waiting for him in his bedroom, spread out like a decadent chocolate and honey dessert came unbidden to his mind. She'd be anticipating his arrival home after a hard day of work, eager to submit to his desires, to be completely his. Suddenly the idea of going home to an empty house didn't seem so appealing.

An hour later he was still unable to concentrate on his work, so he called Sara Florentine to see if Ms. Roa had contacted her yet.

"Hello, Isaac," Sara said in her cultured purr. "How did your meeting with Ms. Roa go?"

"I'm afraid I might have scared her off." He sighed and spun his chair to face the windows looking out over the Capitol in the distance. "Has she called you yet?"

"No, she hasn't. What did you do to frighten her?"

"Well, I offered to be her Master, and she immediately assumed I wanted to have sex with her in exchange for the job."

"Oh dear. That is a rather big mess-up. Did you try to explain to her what you meant?"

"I did, but she wasn't really listening to me. I asked her to call you when she gets home."

"And you want me to smooth things over." She sighed. "Isaac, darling, you need to take things slow with Lucia. She isn't like the women you normally cat around with."

He took offense to that. "I don't cat around."

"Yes, you do. I've never seen you with any woman for more than three weeks. In the past six months, you've gone through ten submissives at Wicked."

He snorted. "Keeping tabs on me?"

"No, but I'm the shoulder they come to cry on when you break up with them."

A twinge of guilt tightened his gut. "Before I play with anyone, I always let them know, as politely as possible, that I'm not looking for anything long-term or a relationship. It's not like I go out, grab some innocent submissive, and rob her of her chastity, then break her heart. My submissives always agree to my terms."

"Why are men so foolish about love?" He started to protest, but she cut him off. "Here is what I suggest. Back off on the request to be her temporary Master. Tell her instead that wearing your collar at Wicked is for her protection, that if the Doms there believe she belongs to you, they will leave her alone. Make it about protection, not possession."

"That makes sense." He stood from his chair and cracked his neck. "I have a meeting to go to, Sara. If Ms. Roa contacts you, could you put in a good word for me?"

"I will. Don't worry, Isaac. I think she'll come around."

"I'm not worried," he said with a grumble.

"Sure you aren't, dear. I'll stop by your office and call Lucia from there. That way I don't have to do any back-and-forth between you two."

"Sounds good, Sara."

He hung up and walked over to the window, watching the world beyond with unseeing eyes. The only image his mind would let him see was Lucia, poised in the doorway to his office, a warm breeze in an otherwise cold and sterile day.

He was in so much trouble.

Chapter Two

Lucia kicked the door to her apartment closed with a muttered oath. She tossed her briefcase onto the counter separating her tiny kitchen from her miniscule living room and removed her heels before chucking them through the bedroom door. On the subway ride home she'd been propositioned for sex three times and groped once. The groper soon regretted his action when she stomped on his foot with her heel.

Her head pounded, her feet ached, and she wanted to call her *madre* to complain about her day, but explaining to her very Catholic mother the situation she found herself in just wasn't going to happen. She tried calling her best friend, Chloe, while she took off her jacket, but there was no answer. A quick glance at the clock above the long ago bricked-up fireplace showed it was still early afternoon.

Too many thoughts and emotions were whirling around in her head, and she couldn't focus on any of them. After rooting around in her almost empty refrigerator, she found her last emergency beer stashed behind a gallon of milk. After twisting the top of her bottle of Tecate with a practiced motion, she sipped at the smooth beer with a sigh. She wandered toward the door leading to her balcony, the main reason she rented this small, cramped third-floor apartment.

Before opening the sliding glass door, she put on the knee-length sweater and warm boots she kept next to the door. She slid the glass door open and stepped out onto her terrace, then took a deep breath of the chilly air. A wrought-iron chair sat next to a mismatched table that looked all too bare in the late winter months. During the summer she decorated her porch until it almost exploded with floral colors. And for Christmas she wound lights through the white-painted iron bars of the porch railing along with some greenery. Most of the people living in the apartment building were elderly, so they appreciated her efforts to brighten the place up. Unfortunately, at the beginning of January, she really didn't have anything to decorate for.

Unless she decorated for Valentine's Day, which in her present mood was not going to happen.

She took a deep drink of her beer, trying to ignore the cold wind blowing up the edge of her sweater. Her anger still burned in her chest, and she could practically hear her brothers teasing her about her hot temper. Regret mixed with irritation, and she took another drink, trying to ignore the little voice telling her she just messed up, big-time.

I work my ass off in the hopes of getting one big break. Now I finally got that break, and I act like an immature girl who's never had sex. So those people like that kind of thing, no big deal. It's not like I'm scared or anything. Just because the thought of Isaac tying me up and doing wicked things with me has my panties soaked only proves my terrible taste in men.

The wind blew a drift of snow off the porch above her, and it fell like glittering sand through the air, swirling on the currents of breeze reaching between the buildings. Okay, so maybe she should have heard him out, but she'd been so sure he'd been propositioning her that her temper had slipped its leash, and he had gotten a taste of who her brothers liked to call "Loco Lucy."

She closed her eyes and leaned back against the brick wall next to her patio door, the coldness slowly leeching through her sweater and stealing her warmth. Dammit, she needed this job, desperately, and more importantly, she needed to pay her workers. The guys who did all of the organizing and maintenance of her supplies down at her warehouse worked hard, and they deserved more than she had to give. It was only because of the recession that she could find skilled workers at an affordable price, way less than they were worth.

The seamstress, the baker, and the liquor company were all getting impatient for her to settle up her debts. She did not want to gain a reputation as a planner who didn't pay on time. The job with Mr. O'Keefe paid an advance of one hundred thousand dollars cash for party supplies; that amounted to nine times as much as she'd ever made on an event. It was a staggering amount of money to her, a life-changing amount of money. If she took this job, she could write all her vendors checks tonight, but at what personal cost?

It wasn't like she wasn't trying to raise enough money on her own. She labored all night at her parents' restaurant as a waitress. Then early in the morning, she'd wake up, head to her warehouse and begin working the phones and Internet, trying to get word out there about her company. Then there was the bill on her office in a seedy warehouse across town for the quarterly payment for rent and utilities. The only way she could cover it would be to sell the solid gold cross her parents had given her for her fifteenth birthday, something that would break her dad's heart.

When she went to take another drink of the beer, she sighed as nothing more than a few drops hit her tongue.

Out of beer, out of money, and out of luck.

The faint sound of her phone ringing came through the glass, and she quickly ran back inside, hoping it was a new client. When she saw Mrs. Florentine's cell phone number, she snatched it up, eager to find out what the hell her mentor had been thinking. "Hello, Mrs. Florentine."

"Lucia, I'm glad I caught you. How did your meeting go?"

"It went great. Other than the part where Mr. O'Keefe said that he wanted me to be his party planning sex slave."

Mrs. Florentine laughed, and Lucia gritted her teeth. "Did he really say that? Those exact words?"

"Did you really send me on a job interview to throw a Valentine's Day party for a BDSM club?"

"Yes, I did. And I thought you would handle it better than this."

"He wants me to be his slave!"

"Did he say slave?"

She leaned her hip against her kitchen counter. "No, not those exact words. He wants me to be his subservient."

"Submissive?"

"Yeah, that."

"Darling, he is hardly asking you to be a sex slave. He is extending his protection to you within the club."

Her spine stiffened. "I don't need anyone to protect me. I know how to handle myself."

"I'm explaining this badly. Lucia, Isaac called me after you left. He is very upset that you went away with the wrong impression and would like to clarify a few things with you. Would you be so kind as to give him a chance to explain?"

Part of her wanted to give this a go, to see how far she could take it. The other part said if she went around these people, she'd be labeled a slut and someone who would have sex for a contract. Then again, when she really thought about it, she didn't give a fuck what other people thought.

They didn't pay her bills, they didn't live her life, and they didn't have the right to judge her.

"Lucia?"

"Yes, I'm here. Did Mr. O'Keefe clarify things to you?"

"Yes, he did, but this is not high school. If you want to know what a man has to say, you need to talk to him yourself."

Chagrined, Lucia sat in the faded mauve chair next to the bricked-over fireplace and curled her feet beneath her. "Oh God, no, don't put him on the line!"

"Lucia, just talk to the man." Just the way Mrs. Florentine said her name made her feel silly, like she was a flighty girl.

"Okay, fine. I'll talk to him."

"Good, here he is."

"Wait. What?" No, no, Mrs. Florentine couldn't have called her from his office.

Oh God.

"Hello, Ms. Roa. Sara, Mrs. Florentine, has left the room, so our conversation is strictly between us. Please feel free to speak your mind."

Isaacs's smooth voice made her whole body tighten with a delicious wave of desire even as embarrassment burned her face. "Hello, Mr. O'Keefe, and thank you, I will."

"I'm so sorry about the misunderstanding earlier. To tell you the truth, you caught me off guard, something that doesn't normally happen to me."

"I'm ready to listen to what you have to say now." Pride filled her at how steady her voice was when inside she was in the middle of a panic attack.

"Excellent."

His voice warmed considerably, and she almost giggled. What the hell was wrong with her? Even talking to the man on the phone was making her into a simpleton. "Before you start, can I tell you something?"

"Of course."

"Let me be honest with you, Mr. O'Keefe. If this is going to work, we need to be honest with each other, correct?"

"Yes, I agree."

She closed her eyes and took a deep breath. "Okay. I'm going to be on the level with you. I know that if I can land this party, I will be able to finally pay my employees what they are worth instead of what I can afford to pay them. If learning about something kinky is what I have to do, well, shoot, I'm glad I'm the boss and can't get fired for inappropriate behavior." Her heart hammered, and her palms slicked with sweat, but she pushed on. "I never feel more alive or happier than when I'm making someone else happy. I love looking out into a crowd and knowing they are having a good time because of me, because of what I did. Party planning is more than a job for me, Mr. O'Keefe. This is my dream."

There was silence on his end except for the faint sound of his breath.

"Mr. O'Keefe?"

"You'd better start calling me Isaac."

"Pardon me?"

"If I'm going to teach you about BDSM in six weeks, we'd better get started tonight."

"Tonight? What are we starting tonight?"

"I agree to your terms."

"My terms?"

"Yes. You said you are willing to learn, and I am willing to teach you. I want you to think of this more as a partnership than a boss and employee relationship. Please feel free to speak your mind around me. I value your opinion, Lucia. If I didn't, I wouldn't be hiring you, no matter what Mrs. Florentine wants."

"Okay, I can do that." A small amount of tension left her body, and she leaned farther into the chair. She frowned and sat up straighter. "I'm still not having sex with you, partners or not."

He chuckled. "I never said you were. I won't do anything to you that you don't ask me for, and no matter how much you beg, I'm not going to fuck you." His deep laugh made her libido perk up. "By the way, around my friends and partners I have a rather foul mouth. Please forgive me."

"No fucking problem." She let out a giggle that sounded a bit hysterical. Oh God, what had she just agreed to?

"Just so you know, your time at the club will be as a bartender instead of a guest."

She felt strangely disappointed. Not that she'd really wanted him to whisk her off into the night and do bad things with her, but bartending seemed so normal.

"Oh, okay."

"It's only because you have to pass a background check before you can get into the private areas of the club. Plus I thought it might be better to take things slowly to give you time to adjust to the water before I threw you into the deep end."

"I feel like I'm already in the deep end, and it's filled with sharks."

He laughed, and the knot in her stomach loosened a bit. "Don't worry. I don't bite."

She flushed and tapped her foot against the floor. "I appreciate that. If I may ask, now that we're working together, why are you going to all this effort to get me to work for you? Surely there is someone who does both event planning and knows BDSM."

He sighed. "Mrs. Florentine, your business mentor and co-owner of Wicked, fancies herself a bit of a matchmaker. I fear her intentions on sending you to me weren't only professional but personal as well. It wouldn't hurt my chances at becoming a member of Wicked's board of directors if the wife of the chairman of the board is happy with me."

She groaned and covered her face with her hands. "Matchmaking? I should have known something was up. Mrs. Florentine is always harping on me to balance work with pleasure and get a boyfriend." She pulled her hands away with a horrified expression. "Oh God, Mrs. Florentine belongs to your club! Please tell me I won't have to watch her have sex."

He busted out laughing. "Oh hell no. While we do have some exhibitionists and voyeur members, most of our members prefer to keep their sexual escapades confined to our private theme rooms. For which I am very thankful." His voice lowered, and her panties got wet—well, wetter. "The most I will do in public is kiss my submissive. All of her charms, all of her beauty belongs to me."

She nervously licked her lips and became distracted by thoughts of kissing him. "When do we start?"

"Are you free all night? It takes a bit to get to the club, and I want to spend enough time with you there that you get a good feel for it."

"Yes." She'd have to bribe her sister to take her shift at the restaurant, but it would be well worth it to see Isaac again. No, wait, not see Isaac. She was excited to see the club where she'd finally get her big break.

That excuse sounded as flimsy as public restroom toilet paper even to her.

"This will of course be paid training to compensate you

for your time. I'm going to e-mail over a bunch of forms. Do you think you can get them filled out by five p.m.?"

"What type of forms?"

"Standard nondisclosure forms. You don't really think the most powerful people in DC would attend a BDSM club without some type of protection? The last thing a senator wants to see is a video of his naked ass being flogged by a dominatrix on YouTube. It might hurt his reelection chances."

She grinned. "That makes sense. Yeah, I'll fill them out as soon as I get off the phone with you."

"I've sent my personal assistant instructions on what to get for an outfit for you. Will you be around later today to accept a delivery?"

"What kind of outfit? And how do you know where I live?" Visions of cheesy leather strap outfits with her ass hanging out came to mind, and she winced.

"Don't worry. You'll be covered from neck to ankle, and you will look amazing. I know where you live because I have your application with your address on it. Will you be at your home tonight?"

She felt silly for being so defensive, but this whole conversation had thrown her off-kilter. "Why?"

"Because I'm going to pick you up tonight, and it would be helpful if you were home when I arrive."

Heat rushed to her cheeks. She thunked her head against the back of the chair. "That sounds lovely. I mean, yes, I'll see you then. At my house, where I'll be." Maybe all the blushing had caused brain damage. That's why she was babbling.

He coughed, and it sounded suspiciously like a muffled laugh. "Excellent. How does eight sound to you?"

"That's fine." There, she was proud of herself for sounding once again like the mature professional woman that she was.

"I'll see you then."

"Oh, yes. That would be wonderful." She inwardly groaned at how breathy and flaky she sounded. Striving to regain her footing, she made sure her words were calm and even as she said, "Thank you again for this opportunity, Mr. O'Keefe."

"Isaac."

She smiled, and his name rolled off her tongue like honey. "Isaac."

CHAPTER THREE

Lucia's best friend, Chloe, grabbed the end of the black bra dangling from Lucia's grip and tried to pull it away. "You can't wear underwear with that outfit."

With a growl Lucia tugged the bra back. "I'm not going out in public without a bra on!"

Chloe jerked the lingerie hard enough so Lucia had to let go or lose a finger. "You're right, you're not going out in public. You're going to super awesome sex club, and you get to wear this super awesome—"

"You mean super slutty," Lucia muttered.

"Outfit," Chloe finished with a wide smile.

They both looked at the outfit in question lying spread out on Lucia's queen-size bed. True to Isaac's word, he'd sent her a getup that would cover her from neck to ankle. He hadn't mentioned it would be a catsuit made out of skintight black latex.

"How am I even supposed to put this thing on? I'll need a bottle of baby oil to slide into it."

"Actually you need to dust yourself down with baby powder first." Chloe tossed back her short blonde hair with an exaggerated movement. "I do happen to know a bit about BDSM."

Lucia snorted. "I'm sure all the kindergarten teachers

at your school like it rough."

Chloe flopped back onto Lucia's mattress. "One of my old boyfriends decided to be a condom for Halloween one year. His outfit was made up of the same stuff as your catsuit, and we had to cover him in baby powder before he put it on."

Lucia picked up the sparkly silver waist corset and shook it at Chloe. "How am I supposed to be able to breathe in this thing?"

"Oh, stop your bitching and put it on already. Your date will be here soon."

She shot Chloe a murderous glare and grabbed the catsuit off the bed. "He's not my date. He's my business partner."

"Sure he is. I Googled him while you were in the shower. He is panty-melting hot and worth like a bazillion dollars."

"I'm not—" She gritted her teeth as she almost said *dating*. "I'm not working with him because of how hot he is or how many steel mills his family owns or how many times he's been on Washington, DC's most-eligible-bachelor list."

"Six times," Chloe chirped, then giggled. "So he's rich, hot, kinky, and loaded? Girl, if you don't go after him, you must not have one working estrogen cell in your body."

While crossing the length of her small bedroom to her master bath, Lucia ignored Chloe's snickers. What could she really say? That Isaac turned her on more than anyone had in a long time, and the only thing he'd done was shake her hand? That the idea of going anywhere with him put her hormones on a low simmer, but the thought of going to a sex club with him lit her libido on fire?

With a little more effort than necessary, she slammed the door to the bathroom behind her and tossed the clothing onto her sink. She dug around the medicine cabinet and found an old bottle of lavender-scented body powder. After dousing herself in the mixture, she slipped on the smallest G-string she owned and muttered threats against Chloe when she noticed the bra was missing.

After some pulling, stretching, and bending, she finally managed to tug the tight latex suit on all the way and zip up the front. Thankfully it was lined with a layer of ultrathin fabric on the inside, so it didn't pull her skin off as she wiggled everything into place. She actually liked the way it clung to her, almost making her feel like she was being hugged all over her body. Taking a deep breath, she turned to look at herself in the mirror and gaped.

She looked amazing. Well, super slutty, but still amazing. The catsuit stuck to her body like it was painted on, and she could make out the slight bumps of her nipples beneath the black latex. On either side a row of tiny silver rivets ran up her body from her ankle to the inside of her wrist. The only thing she didn't like was how the rounded bump of her belly became more pronounced, but then she remembered the corset. Running a hand down her slick curves, she opened the door and struck a pose.

"Ta-da!"

Chloe sat up and rubbed her eyes. "Holy moly. You look like a high-class porn star."

"Can you help me get into this corset thing, please?"

They both giggled as Chloe helped her cinch her waist into the corset. "Can you breathe?"

She wheezed in reply.

Her best friend loosened a few laces and stepped back with her hands on her hips. "You know, this might be a good look for you. With your waist cinched like that, you have a very 1950s Marilyn Monroe thing going on. You know, if Marilyn was Hispanic and had a bigger butt."

She wiggled her butt at Chloe, then looked in the

mirror above her dresser and smiled. "Hair up or down?"

"Up. Let's give you an *I Dream of Jeannie* ponytail."

Chloe pulled her over to the bed and sat her down before brushing her hair. "You have your cell phone, right? And you'll call me at any time to come get you if you're in trouble?"

"Yes, Mom."

Chloe jerked her hair up with more force than necessary. "You never know these days who is going to turn out to be some kind of psycho killer."

"Weren't you the one just listing off his attributes?"

"True. " Chloe yawned and stretched. "Do you think he likes to smack some ass or have his ass smacked?"

Lucia snorted and grabbed her black stiletto high heels off the end table. The five-inch spikes were dangerous territory for most women, but at five feet three, she'd always worn tall heels to be in the normal height range for women. "I think he's the spanker, not the spankee."

The intercom to her small apartment buzzed, and both women exchanged an excited look. With Lucia still fumbling with securing the ankle strap of her shoes, Chloe beat her to the intercom. With a grin she pressed the Talk button and said in a singsong voice, "Who is it?"

"Isaac O'Keefe."

Lucia elbowed Chloe away from the intercom. "Come on up. I'm on the second floor, and my apartment is the last one on the left. There's a floral wreath on the door."

She tried to push Chloe into the guest bathroom, but her friend managed to wiggle away with a laugh. "Hey! I promise I'll behave."

"Just sit on the couch and don't say a word."

Chloe bounced onto her small lilac-gray sectional and pantomimed zipping her lips. After giving her friend one final glare, Lucia turned to the door and tried to slow down her suddenly hammering heart. Good Lord, she hadn't been this worked up about a guy in forever. Maybe it had been so long since she'd had sex that her body was going to make her have it by sending out nymphomaniac rushes of hormones.

A knock sounded on the door, and she opened it so quick she caught Isaac on the other side with his hand still raised. He stared at her from the top of her head all the way down to her toes and back up again. Then he smiled, and her nipples hardened into very visible rock-hard buds. Dressed in another impeccable black suit, this time with a pale silver tie, he looked like he'd stepped off of some French runway.

"Hey!" Chloe yelled from over her shoulder. "Why isn't he in latex? Or better yet, leather pants. Seems only fair if you have to dress up like BDSM Barbie, he should be your Kinky Ken."

Lucia gave Isaac a weak smile. "Let me grab my purse and jacket, and we will be off."

Isaac's lips twitched, but he nodded. "Of course."

Chloe came up behind her and dodged the not so subtle elbow Lucia threw her way. "Hmm, you are a nice tall drink of water. Love your eyes. They remind me of a Siberian husky."

"I'm so sorry about this." Lucia grabbed her purse from the table next to the door and jerked her crimson trench coat out of the closet. "Chloe was dropped on her head at birth, and she used to eat paint chips."

To Isaac's credit he didn't crack a smile. "Poor girl."

"Indeed. Say good night to the nice gentleman, Chloe."

Chloe grinned and waved. "Have fun, and remember, if you're a psycho and you hurt my friend, I'll spend the rest of my life hunting you down."

With a smile he held his hand out to Chloe, and she placed her palm in his with a hot blush. Isaac bent and raised Chloe's hand to his mouth. He briefly brushed his lips across her skin, and Lucia's best friend's blush went from pink to stop-sign red. "It has been a pleasure meeting you, Chloe. Lucia is lucky to have a friend who cares so much."

He released her hand, and Chloe dragged in a deep breath. "Holy crap, Lucia. I hope you're on birth control, because this guy is lethal."

Mortified, Lucia closed the door on a stunned Chloe and sighed. "Once again, please let me apologize. You know that filter people have in their head that tells them not to say something? Well, Chloe's is broken, and she is way more honest than most people are comfortable with. It makes her a great kindergarten teacher because she can relate so well to the way kids think, but it throws most people over four feet tall for a loop."

"I find her honesty refreshing. The business world is littered with kiss asses and backstabbers, so hearing someone say what they think instead of what they think you want them to say is nice."

They made their way down the hall of her second-floor apartment to the front door. She kept her coat clutched tight in the hopes none of her elderly neighbors would be looking out their windows. On Thursday afternoons she usually had tea with the old lady across the hall and her friends. If they saw her tonight, she knew they'd ask about it during tea, then tease her mercilessly with stories of the naughty things they did when they were young. The old women were like her adopted, perverted aunts.

"Let's take the stairs. It's quicker."

He glanced down at her feet. "You can climb stairs in those?"

"Honey, I can do a lot of things in these shoes." She realized how utterly dirty that sounded and flushed when he gave her a wicked grin. "I didn't mean it like that."

His laughter echoed as they entered the stairwell. "I'm sure you didn't."

She wanted to glare at him, but if she turned around, she might bust her ass on these stairs.

When they reached the front door, she inwardly groaned at the sight of the black limousine parked in front of her apartment complex. He held the door open for her, and she stepped out into the chilly late-winter air, her breath puffing white in the glare of the sodium security lights. A quick glance behind her confirmed a great deal of the windows facing the parking circle were filled with curious faces watching them. Mrs. Goldbitz on the second floor actually waved when she noticed Lucia looking.

Lucia waved back, then made a shooing gesture, which everyone pretty much ignored.

A good-looking dark-haired man in a chauffeur's uniform opened the door to the limo with a smile. "Good evening, Ms. Roa. My name is Marcus, and if you need anything, please let me know."

"Thank you." She carefully stepped into the limo and chose a seat on the long bench that took up one side. The car leaned slightly as Isaac got in and took a seat at the back. He blew into his hands and smiled. "Thank you for joining me this evening. I realize this is a rather unconventional job, and I appreciate your willingness to think outside the box."

She shifted as the limo pulled away from the curb. "I'd say this outfit is rather outside the box."

He grinned. "Compared to what most people wear, you're dressed like a nun." He leaned over and pulled a small black box she hadn't noticed out of a compartment in the beverage area lining the opposite side of the limo. "By the way, I thought you might like this as well."

Curious, she took the box and lifted the lid. Inside lay a beautiful half mask shaped like a cat's face on a bed of red silk. It would cover the upper portion of her face while leaving the bottom exposed. "Is there a costume party tonight?"

"No, this is to give you some anonymity. Some of our members wear similar masks to keep their identity a secret. However, most members want to be seen and noticed. Getting accepted into Wicked is harder than getting into the Illuminati and considered a great honor among our members."

"That makes sense." She turned the box so the black sparkles lining the eyeholes shimmered in the passing lights outside of the limo.

"The mask is made out of a special foam that will conform to the shape of your face, so it should be rather comfortable."

Intrigued, she lifted the mask and noted there wasn't any string to hold it on her head. "How does this work?"

"Here, let me help you."

He scooted over, and their knees touched as he leaned forward. Just that little bit of contact started a tingle low in her stomach. When he took the mask from her unresisting grasp, she had to fight the urge to brush her fingers over his hand, to feel the slight dusting of hair beneath her fingertips.

"Close your eyes. It fits better that way."

She complied and almost sighed at his gentle touch pressing the mask to her skin. With his wrist by her nose, she could smell his crisp cologne and the slight sent of soap. He continued to stroke and press the mask onto her face, tracing the line of her cheekbones and molding it to the curve of her brow. Neither of them said anything, and when he finally pulled back, she was glad she'd worn underwear, because her panties were already wet with desire, and all he'd done was touch her face. She had to get ahold of herself. At this rate she'd be on her knees begging him to take her before they even reached the club. It was embarrassing how easily she got revved up around him. Really, he wasn't all that. So he was handsome, sophisticated, smart, and so fucking sexy her teeth hurt. That didn't mean she had to act like a cat in heat.

She opened her eyes and found him staring intently at her. Nervous, she ran her fingertips over the mask. "How does it look?"

"Well, I haven't seen the full effect of the outfit yet, but I'm pretty sure we're going to need you to wear something to keep me from having to beat off the single Doms."

"Doms? You mean dominants? Like the guys that get off on being called Master?"

"Did a little research this afternoon?"

She grinned and liked how the mask moved with her face. "Let's just say I hope my mom never sees the search history on my computer and some of my new bookmarks."

"Good, then you'll know what this is." He reached into his pocket and pulled out a black velvet ribbon with a small gold disk dangling from the end of it.

"Um, I'm not sure what that is."

"It's my personal collar." He must have seen her panicked look, because he smiled. "No, I'm not claiming you as my submissive or anything like that. At least not in private. In public this will keep the Doms off you…or at least in theory it should."

"This is doesn't mean you own me or anything like that, right?"

His pale blue eyes glittered in the passing lights, and his smile seemed almost predatory. "No, that collar doesn't mean you belong to me."

Their fingers touched as she plucked the medallion from his hand. Inscribed on the gold circlet was the simple word Mine. She couldn't help but giggle as she tied the velvet ribbon around her neck. "Seriously? 'Mine'?"

He grinned, and her heart fluttered. "Keeps it simple. Can I ask you a question?"

She snorted and fingered the medallion. "Sure."

"Do you really speak the five languages you have listed on your résumé?"

She looked up at him in surprise, having expected a more intimate question. "Yes. French, Italian, Spanish, English, and passable Portuguese."

"I must say I'm impressed. Why so many?"

"Because I want to do international parties, and I would love to travel." She settled back into the seat and continued to stroke the medallion. "Plus it allows me to speak with the staff of various decorating and catering companies. I can calm down a French chef and at the same time tell the Italian florist exactly what I want."

"Very smart." He glanced down at his watch, a strand of his dark hair falling over his forehead. "We should be arriving at the club soon. Let me tell you what I have planned tonight."

Hot, kinky sex with you? her libido whispered hopefully. "Okay."

He laughed. "How long has it been since you last bartended?"

"Last week at my family's restaurant."

"Good. I just wanted to make sure you were up to making a variety of drinks."

A little tingle of nerves moved up her spine. "Will you be nearby?" God, she sounded so needy, but the thought of being alone in a sex club for the first time almost sent her running into the street.

"Yes, I'll be hanging out at the bar with you. I won't always be right in front of you, but I'll be nearby if you have any problems or need anything clarified. This will be a good opportunity for you to get a feel for the club and its members as well as staff. Do you have any questions?"

"About a million." She gave him a rueful smile. "Is this club high protocol?"

"You have been doing your homework." He gave her a pleased smile that caused an unexpected warmth in her belly. "We leave that up to the members. Some do insist on the whole rule set of high protocol while others could give a crap. Just remember that as far as the club members are concerned, you are my submissive, and you follow whatever rules I dictate. That doesn't mean you should be rude, but please let me know right away if anyone is giving you any trouble." He leaned forward, and his voice took on a dark tone. "While I may not be your real Master, I will look after you and protect you as if I am."

Normally she would have been offended and made some snarky remark about being able to protect herself, but something about the way Isaac said it made her feel all warm and glowy inside. "Got it."

"And if you are curious about anything, please let me know. I'll do my best to...educate you."

Her heart thumped against her breastbone at the sensual tone to his words. Then again, he could probably read the back of a box of cake mix, and it would sound carnal. She wasn't sure if he meant more than what he said, so she settled for a simple reply. "Thanks."

"Oh, one more thing. Do you want me to use your real name?"

"Um, what do you think?"

He shrugged. "I don't bother to hide who I am or what I enjoy. If anyone has a problem with it, they've been told to fuck off a long time ago. But I'm in a position where I can do that pretty much without fear of retribution. With you I might err on the side of caution and suggest a nickname for now."

She traced the line of her mask. "How about Cat?"

"You seem more like Kitten to me." He must have caught her narrow-eyed look, because he held up his hands. "I meant that as a compliment. Cats are so aloof and jaded. You remind me more of a kitten. Cute, inquisitive, and unafraid of the world."

She blushed and looked down at her hands. Good Lord, he called her cute, and she got all flustered and giggly inside. So much for the urbane and sophisticated persona she'd been trying to cultivate. "Well, when you put it that way, it doesn't sound so bad. Kitten it is."

The car slowed to a stop, and her mouth went dry. She leaned back to look out the windows, but she couldn't see much beyond some type of parking lot and a bunch of trees. "Are we here?"

"Yes, welcome to Club Wicked, Kitten."

She fidgeted with the fit of the corset beneath her jacket. "This thing was not made for sitting down comfortably."

"I'll set you up with an account at the costume shop my friend's wife owns. You might meet her tonight. Her name is Laurel, and she's about five-five with red curly hair and a wicked sense of humor. Oh, and she's a submissive, so feel free to ask her about the lifestyle." The shadow of the driver moved past the window, and Isaac leaned closer until he was almost within kissing distance. "Once we are inside I will become a little more…demanding with you. It is in part of the role I play as a Dominant, but also because I find myself rather protective of you." He brushed the edge of her mask where it met the skin of her cheek, and she almost moaned.

A moment later the chauffer opened the car door, and the bitterly cold January air blasted through the warmth of the limo's interior. Isaac stepped out and offered her his hand. She placed her palm against his and hoped the sudden stiffening of her nipples would be attributed to the chill. A quick glance down showed they indeed stuck out, and every little bump was visible behind the latex.

Isaac made a pained sound and pulled her jacket closed. "I've changed my mind. We'll find you something else to wear."

She stepped away from the car and tugged her jacket out of his hands. "I'm sorry. I thought it looked okay."

"Okay?" He gave her a wicked smirk that looked right at home on his handsome face. "You're going to cause a riot. Just wait and see."

Chapter Four

A couple of hours later, Lucia found herself behind the most fabulous bar of the most fabulous place she'd ever been in.

Kinky but fabulous.

Though she'd only seen the public lounge and the staff area so far, she still had gotten more than an eyeful of both seminaked men and women strolling around as if it were the most natural thing in the world. A series of golden silk couches gathered in small circles spanned the room that she was in for the night, the Louis the XIV Bar. True to its namesake, this portion of the club boasted gold everywhere in a stunning display of warmth and wealth. Floor-to-ceiling windows in between golden columns made up one portion of the room, while the opposite side had massive mirrors reflecting the scene before her in a variety of angles.

The arched ceiling overhead was painted with classical figures doing rather naughty things. Here a voluptuous woman knelt on a cloud as she gave a man clothed in a white toga oral sex. Next to them a group of three women twined together in a mass of long hair and plush limbs. Elaborate chandeliers hung down, throwing a forgiving light over the crowd. They needed this kind of lighting in the dressing rooms at her local mall. It made everyone look good.

But not as good as the dark-haired man in an impeccable black suit smiling at her.

She made a gesture of closing her open mouth, and Isaac laughed before lifting his drink to her. Sunny, the other bartender, was handling the busier area where he sat while Lucia took the occasional waitress coming into the room with a drink order from the private area of the club they called the Dark Shadows. Evidently it was modeled after a famous dungeon in Italy where people had been tortured during the Inquisition. Sunny had quickly assured her that no one was getting tortured in that room who didn't want it, and they weren't using burning-hot pokers or anything like that.

She leaned over the bar every time the door opened, but all she could catch in the reflection of the mirrors was a wooden rack holding what looked like a variety of whips. She swallowed hard at the thought of how much it must hurt and wondered how anyone could ever get into that. Now if Isaac wanted to tie her up and spank her, gently, she could definitely give it a try.

A man cleared his throat, and Lucia jumped, then flushed. "I'm sorry, I was daydreaming. How can I help you?"

On the other side of the marble bar top stood a supercute dark-haired guy in a pair of leather pants. His pouty lower lip was pierced, and he was remarkably pale with skin like ivory. She immediately thought of Chloe's comments about cute guys in leather pants and had to bite back a smile. His green eyes glowed with mischief as he leaned forward and said in a deep voice while looking at her breasts, "Any daydreams I can help come true?"

She rolled her eyes and placed a hand on her hip. Men had been drooling over her breasts since she developed them, and it annoyed the shit out of her. True, this outfit kinda invited it, but that didn't mean she couldn't redirect their attention. "My eyes are up here, buddy."

He cocked his head and gave her an innocent look. "I was admiring your corset, ma'am."

A tall redheaded woman dressed like a naughty French maid hip checked him. "You're barking up the wrong tree, Adam. This one belongs to Isaac."

Lucia leaned over and fished out the little medallion that had slipped into the V above her breasts and held it up. "Yep, taken. Sorry."

Adam gave her a frown that he must have practiced in the mirror, because it made him look so cute. "Oh. My mistake."

"It's okay. I'm actually an event planner that will be doing Wicked's Valentine's Day party, but I'm trying to learn the lay of the land tonight." The smile dropped off his face, and he gave her a decidedly unfriendly look. She flushed, confused by his sudden change in demeanor. "Um, can I get you a drink? I really am a good bartender."

He swallowed and gave her a forced smile. "No, that's okay."

The other woman patted his back. "Are you all right, Adam? You're looking a little pale—well, paler than usual."

He shook his head, a lock of his dark hair falling over his eyes. "Thanks, but I'm okay. I forgot to eat dinner tonight, so I'm a little light-headed." He regained his composure and gave Lucia a flirtatious grin. "I don't suppose you have anything for me to eat?"

A hot blush burned her ears. "I think we have some peanuts around here. Or I can order you something from the kitchen."

He gave a dramatic sigh. "I don't suppose you're a switch?"

The redhead snorted. "The only thing that's going to get switched is your ass if you don't watch yourself. Take a look down yonder bar." They all turned, and Lucia raised her eyebrows in surprise at the dark look Isaac was giving Adam. "If you want to give his arm a try, you keep flirting with his pet. Plus I don't think Lady Morgana would be too happy offering your skills."

Adam held up his hands and backed away. "Please don't say anything to her. I was just joking. Besides, I see what you mean about Master Isaac." With that he turned and sauntered farther down the hallway to where other theme rooms were. Both women watched him walk away and sighed in appreciation.

The redhead held out her hand. "Hi, my name is Laurel. I'm assuming you're Isaac's Kitten?"

Remembering that she needed to play the role of Isaac's submissive, she nodded. "That's me."

Laurel grinned and leaned against the bar. "I need a magnum of the 99 Cristal and three champagne glasses."

"Right away." She went over to the massive champagne cooler and rooted through the racks of bottles looking for the one Laurel wanted. Goodness, there had to be tens of thousands of dollars' worth of champagne here. She grabbed the right bottle and turned back to the bar.

Laurel took it from her with a friendly smile and handed Lucia her membership card to swipe. "So Isaac mentioned you're really, really new to the lifestyle."

With a dry chuckle, Lucia nodded, then swiped her card and handed it back. "You could say I'm taking a crash course." She picked up one of the crystal champagne glasses and gave it a quick rubdown with a clean cloth.

"While I can understand why he dressed you the way he did, and you look fucking fantastic by the way, I don't think he intentionally meant for you to come off as a Domme. Am I wrong in assuming you aren't very interested in paddling any cute boy's ass? Or girls?"

Lucia laughed and placed another glass on the tray. "No. That really doesn't do anything for me."

"But being paddled does?"

"Oh, I've never been paddled. I've been spanked before, and it was really hot, but we were both drunk at the time."

Laurel shot a narrow-eyed look in Isaac's direction. "Pushing you kind of fast, isn't he? I mean, you've never done anything kinkier than a spanking, and he throws you in the middle of Wicked dressed like that. Need me to talk to him?"

"No," she said quickly. "Thank you, but no. I promise you he didn't drag me here against my will or anything like that. He's a great guy, and he's been nothing but nice to me."

Laurel rolled the stem of the glass between her fingers. "He must really like and trust you."

"Why do you say that?"

"Because of the Rick James he pulled to get you in here."

Lucia shook her head. "Did I fall down the rabbit hole at some point?"

The other woman's laughter was warm and husky. "What I'm trying to say is he put his ass on the line to get you in to this club. We call it a Rick James because the singer tried to get in here once in the eighties, and he threw an epic fit when no one recognized him."

"So Isaac threw a fit to get me in here?"

"Well, his version of a fit. He had to get all threatening and scary about what he'd do if they didn't let you in."

Embarrassment flooded Lucia. She covered her face with her hands and mumbled through her fingers, "Shit."

Laurel patted her on the head. "Don't worry, Kitten.

As long as you do what he says, you'll be okay. Master Isaac is a good man, and he deserves a good woman. You're the first sub he's ever brought here with him, and to me that speaks volumes about your character."

"I...that is...thanks." She wished one of the chandeliers would fall from the ceiling and crush her, saving her from this uncomfortable situation. "But look, I'm not out to hurt him. He is a great guy, and I want this to work."

"Just remember, even if something he asks you to do seems weird, don't argue in public with him about it unless he's hurting you or you have to go to the bathroom."

"Thanks for the advice." She swore she could feel Isaac's gaze burning into her back. Did he know they were talking about him?

Laurel took the last glass from her with a small smile. She leaned forward and motioned Lucia closer. "For what it's worth, every time I've come in here, he's been watching you. I've never seen him so focused on anyone before, not even his ex-wife."

She glanced over her shoulder, and sure enough, Isaac was watching them. He raised one eyebrow and shook his empty glass.

"Uh-oh, busted," Laurel said with a laugh. "I hope he doesn't talk to my Master about me gossiping. He'll strap my ass till it's raw."

Alarmed, she leaned over to pat Laurel's hand. "I'll make sure he knows you're innocent."

"Please don't." She gave a mock shudder that sent her auburn curls trembling. "I love it when my Master scolds me. It was nice meeting you, Kitten. Now you better go see what your Dom wants before he comes over here and hangs you from the ceiling as a bar ornament."

She took a deep breath and turned away from Laurel, only to find herself caught by Isaac's gaze. He had arched eyebrows, and when he smirked, as he was doing now, he looked downright fuckable. No, no, not fuckable. He looked like her boss, kind of sort of, even though the people who owned the club were actually her bosses, and he was more like an emissary from the world of leather and lace.

Those thoughts didn't cool her down as she approached him. When his gaze locked on her breasts, she put an extra spring in her step, inwardly laughing at the slightly glazed look on his face. Okay, so maybe she was a bit of a hypocrite considering the way she'd told off the last guy who had stared at her breasts, but when Isaac watched her, something deep inside her soul purred with pleasure.

Her smooth glide was interrupted by an ill-placed napkin stuck to her heel. With a low growl, she leaned over and tugged, then tossed the offending paper into the garbage can beneath the bar. He wisely didn't laugh when she reached him.

"Could I get a rum and Coke?"

She crossed her arms beneath her breasts, aware she was acting like a total hussy and finding it strangely hard to care. Maybe they pumped some kind of hormone into the air here so everyone felt incredibly horny. It was certainly a better thought than the idea that this man, whom she barely knew, affected her so much.

"Sir, may I have your ticket, please?"

His grin fell, and he leaned forward on the bar. "I must confess, I'm out of tickets. See, I've been busy glaring at everyone getting near you, and it's a rather thirsty task."

She pointed to the sign behind her that clearly stated the drinking rules of the club. "Sorry, but if you want to play in the theme rooms tonight, you can't have any more drinks. Club rules."

"And leave you unattended? I think not."

Even though he wasn't really her man, just playing

the role for their mutual benefit, she couldn't help but feel better knowing he wasn't going to run off with one of the amazingly beautiful subs who had been hitting on him all night. It seemed like every time she looked over, one skinny chick or another was either kneeling next to him, whispering into his ear or some other type of flirting. Every guy she knew would have gone with one of them in a heartbeat, yet Isaac stayed right here with her in what had to be his most boring evening at the bar. Still, her feminine pride insisted she not let on as to how much he affected her.

She rested her hip on the edge of the bar and lowered her voice. "Why don't you just brand me on my forehead so everyone can instantly see who I belong to?"

He smirked, and she wanted to kiss him so badly she was contemplating grabbing him by the back of the head and laying one on him. Though, considering he was the dominant in their *fake but feeling more real by the second* relationship, it might be in her best interest to beg him for one. Then again, Laurel thought her Dom being angry with her was a good thing.

Weird.

Isaac laughed and rubbed a hand through his dark hair, mussing it and making him look a little more approachable. "No, if I wanted to do that, I'd brand your gorgeous breasts."

Heat flooded her face, but she tilted her chin up and said in an imperious voice, "Thank you. I grew them myself."

He swirled the melting ice in the bottom of his glass. "So any questions yet?"

"Not really. This is kind of like a social club for people in kinky clothing. From what I saw of the kitchens and prep when Sunny showed me around, it looks much like a high-end restaurant back there. I don't think I'll have any issues with getting the appropriate staff in place. And since the kitchens are isolated from the rest of the club and can only be accessed with a security code on all of the doors leading into the rest of the building, I don't think safety will be that big of a concern."

"Plus we have extra private security guards on all big events to help keep the peace." He tilted his chin toward the sitting area. "We also have guests who bring in their own bodyguards for personal protection."

She looked around, and a thrum of anticipation sped her heart. "If the rest of the club is anything like this, I'll have no problem. What is the crowd going to be like? I mean, it's a Wednesday night, and this place is over half full. The weekends must be insane."

"They are, which is why I like coming during the week. As for Valentine's Day, I'd say we're probably going to have at least twenty-five hundred guests." He gave her that half smile that drove her nuts. "So, are you having fun?"

"I'd be having fun if you weren't scaring away all my clients." She waggled her finger in his face. "You are bad for my business."

To her utter shock, he sat forward and captured her finger between his teeth, his hot breath blowing over her skin. She tried to pull back, but he tightened his grip on it. Holding her gaze, he slowly sucked her finger into his mouth and then slid it back out again. Her finger rested on his firm lower lip. Even remembering to breathe was becoming a struggle. One suck of her finger and she was ready to take him right here, right now. Her pussy was wet and tender, and the way the catsuit pressed into her sex when she bent over was not helping things.

She drew her finger back, and he gave her such a smug smile that her desire faded beneath her ire, but he'd still managed to turn her brain into a puddle of hormones. "I— You— This... I, yeah." She took a deep breath and ordered her brain to function. "Nice men don't suck on strange women's fingers. That's just dirty."

His eyes grew wide, and he roared with laughter, almost falling off his stool. His chest heaved, and he tried to straighten up, but as soon as he met her gaze, he doubled over. One of the men at the other end of the bar came over—a rather cute guy with hints of red in his neatly trimmed beard. He wore a pair of faded jeans that clung to his lean hips and a cream flannel shirt.

The other man smacked Isaac none too gently on the back. "What kind drugs are you on tonight, man? And can I have some?"

Isaac wheezed. "No drugs. I'm a nice guy."

Glaring at Isaac she contemplated the new guy. He definitely had that powerful feel about him that people used when describing Doms. Another word that fit was *charismatic*. Yeah, that described these men. There was something about them, some indefinable quality that screamed dominant. She rather liked it. Remembering how weird Isaac had acted when that guy hit on her, she decided to shut his laughing face up.

Unzipping the front of the catsuit to reveal enough cleavage to make the average man drool, she leaned forward and smiled at the newcomer. "Hi, can I get you anything?"

She let her accent thicken on the last few words, and the man with the beard smiled. "Well, darl'n, that all depends on what's on the menu." He had a faint inflection to his words, she'd guess Texas.

Isaac was still chuckling as he leaned back on his stool. Maybe he would fall, and that would shut him up. She was pissed the floor was probably impeccably clean instead of dirty like he deserved. "I've never done anything of this before, but my wicked fantasies all involve Dominance and submission. You know, forbidden pleasures." She paused, enjoying the way the other man's eyes darkened, and he somehow became more imposing. "I would like to start with someone who knows what he's doing." She cocked her head to the side and licked her lips. "Do you know anyone who would fit the bill?"

Before the other man could respond, Isaac was leaning over the bar and plucking the medallion off her upper chest. He looked at the other man, all traces of mirth gone, and said, "If you'll excuse us, Jesse, I think I need to introduce my pet to some of those forbidden pleasures she's so fond of. Be a friend and jump over the counter for me and grab a bottle of champagne. The good stuff."

Jesse slid across the bar surface, and she had an impression of long, strong legs in denim sliding past her. The moment Jesse touched the ground, he turned and lifted her by the waist onto the counter. Before she could take a breath, Isaac had his hands on her hips and tugged her forward until her swollen core pressed up against his abdomen. God bless him, that man had a six-pack hidden behind his shirt.

He leaned forward and whispered into her ear, "Thank you for playing along." He paused, and his breath warmed her skin, his body so close to hers, and he smelled so good. She could stay here and inhale him like this and float in bliss.

Unable to speak, she moaned low in her throat when he licked the side of her neck, his teeth skimming the surface of her skin with little bites that made her shivery inside. He grabbed her ponytail with one of his hands and wrapped his fist in her long hair. With the makeshift rope of her hair, he held her head at an angle, further exposing her neck to him.

He placed one gentle kiss on her banging pulse, and she arched against his stomach, her hips twitching.

The next moment, he released her hair and stepped back, putting space in between them. She breathed a bit harder than normal, but he appeared unruffled. "Come along, Kitten. You want to learn some forbidden pleasures, and I can't wait to teach them to you."

He lifted her from the bar, allowing her to slide down his front and take note of his very thick erection pressing into her. A woman could have ten kids, and a man that wide would still be wall-to-wall. Maybe he wasn't really aroused. Maybe he was carrying around a water bottle in his pants. She, on the other hand, was practically panting.

Without another word, he turned and motioned for her to follow. Her heels clicked against the wooden floors as she trailed after him. They crossed the room, and it seemed like everyone was looking at them. Then again, if they were men, they were probably watching her boobs bounce all over the place. She shrank down into herself a bit, feeling like a slut. She certainly looked like a slut, acted like a slut—well, she must be a slut.

That thought struck her as both funny and sad at the same time, but it took the curve out of her spine. Fuck it. She wore a mask, and she knew some of the members hadn't bothered to disguise themselves. It really was a collection of DC and Baltimore's highest and brightest. And hottest. She caught the eye of a man she recognized as a major action movie star, Hawk. He had long, shiny black hair and looked to be of Native American ancestry. She never thought celebrities looked as good in real life as he did. He was flawless.

She ran into the muscled wall of Isaac's chest and stumbled. He sighed and shook his head, placing a hand on her lower back to lead her into a waiting elevator cab. With a wicked grin, he took the cold bottle of champagne and rolled it over her buttocks. She screeched and jumped away as the doors to the elevator slid shut.

Rubbing her cold butt, she glared at him. "Okay, seriously, what the fuck was all of that about?"

He shrugged and began to unwrap the champagne

bottle. "Do you like gardens?"

"What?"

"Do you like gardens?"

"I guess so. My grandma had a lovely flower garden. But I'm still mad at you."

"Would you like to drink excellent champagne in the middle of a thousand roses and look at the stars? You're free to yell at me. I just thought we could spend that time relaxing instead. You've been exposed to a great deal in a short amount of time. So let me make up for being a beast and join me for a drink?"

He made it sound so reasonable that her anger deflated a bit. "You were a beast."

"I was."

"Wait, it's like thirty degrees outside. I'll get hypothermia in this outfit."

He laughed and shook his head. "Don't worry. It's in a greenhouse."

The doors to the elevator slid open, and she forgot what she was going to say. Stepping out of the cab was like stepping into a fantasy land. They were on the rooftop of a four-story building. Wicked had to be somewhere outside of DC, because for as far as she could see, there were trees and gently rolling hills with the city lights way off in the distance. The roof itself was a forest with real grass. Well, maybe forest was a stretch, but it was certainly amazing. Most amazing of all was the warmth.

When she looked closer, she could see where the panes of greenhouse glass had been joined together with super thin strips of metal. A faint breeze came from somewhere, so the air was circulated, but if she didn't look hard, it would almost be like being outside. Except she was in a fairy-tale forest high in the sky with a handsome prince.

She mentally gave herself a smack. No, no romantic

nonsense. She didn't care what all those princess movies she'd watched as a kid said. There were no princes in real life. She needed to get her head out of the clouds and back to earth.

Isaac leaned against the door of the elevator, keeping it open. "Shoes off, please."

She nodded and slipped her heels from her feet, putting her shoes on the marble slab right off the elevator. Not waiting for him, she took a step and sank into grass as soft as a baby's blanket. Everything around her smelled like summer even though a crystalline winter moon hung from the sky above them.

"This is amazing, but won't you get in trouble for bringing me here?"

"Actually, Sara, Mrs. Florentine, arranged this." He shrugged and looked a bit uncomfortable. "She's serious about me wooing you and pulling all the stops."

"Woo me?"

"Yes, Sara has rather old-fashioned ideas about how a gentleman should court a lady."

"I'll say. Having a midnight glass of champagne in the middle of a summer forest, in the sky above the trees, while snow is on the ground is *so* old-fashioned."

"What can I say? I think I might be an old-fashioned guy where you're concerned."

A wisp of silvery cloud floated across the moon, slightly dimming its light. She wondered what he meant by being old-fashioned around her. The silly, girlish part of her mind wanted to believe that he may have more feelings for her than he let on, but he'd been very clear about not wanting a relationship. Weren't relationships old-fashioned? Or maybe he just said that in passing, just a play off her response. Most likely he'd meant nothing by it, and she was seeing something that wasn't there. That thought hurt more than it should. She tried to shake off the melancholy, to recapture her joy. Looking around at the amazing garden, it wasn't hard to immerse herself in the moment, to enjoy what she had rather than longing for something romantic and silly.

She laughed and held the bottle of champagne while he rolled his pants up. He turned to look up at her, and his delicious lips curved into a crooked smile that made her heart beat faster. "What?"

He finished rolling the cuff and stood to face her. As her eyes adjusted to the darkness, she marveled at the shadows created on his face, giving him an almost sinister air. Like the evil prince in the fairy-tale garden. He lifted his hand to touch her, then shoved it in his pocket instead. "You know, you look lovely in the moonlight."

"Flattery will get you nowhere, good sir." Her voice came out husky, giving weight to her flippant words.

He only grinned and rolled up his socks while placing his shoes neatly next to her heels.

She surveyed the area and decided which path to take. To the right came the faint sound of water while to the left an enormous hammock with dozens of silk pillows swayed between two trees. Straight ahead was the entrance to what looked like a hedge maze. Delicate purple flowers wreathed the bushes of the maze, and she wasn't sure she'd ever seen the exotic blossoms outside of a book before.

When she wanted to ask a question about the kind of bushes growing here, she found he'd moved up behind her without her knowing. The warmth of his frame burned along her spine. If he touched her, all bets were off. There was no way she could resist him, not after him watching her all night, and especially not after his actions toward her at the bar. The memory of sliding down his hard, masculine frame sent a tremble through her sex. They were both adults, and if he belonged to a club like this, he certainly wasn't a prude. She didn't think she was misreading his attraction to her. Hell, she could practically feel his lust pressing against her, touching her in the most intimate of ways. Her body craved him, and she couldn't think of any reason to fight it.

He moved around to her front and looked down at her before taking the champagne bottle from her unresisting fingers. "Come on, I want to show you something."

Chapter Five

He slipped his fingers into hers and led her to the right toward the sound of falling water. They crossed a grassy space big enough to host a large picnic and went past some erotic statues that probably belonged in a museum instead of Wicked's private collection. As they neared the source of the sound, she began to pick up a marvelous perfume to the air. The colors that burned in the darkness flared to life when they walked around a corner. Then her world took on an almost surreal reality as she stepped into an enchanted garden filled with roses of every description and hue.

Stunned, she whispered, "Places like this don't really exist."

"They do in my world." Isaac let go of her hand and took a step back. "Go ahead. Everyone reacts this way when they first see the roses."

She walked to the center of the massive garden and admired the black marble fountain depicting a circle of women in old-fashioned farm clothes laughing and splashing each other. Water lilies bigger than her hand floated at the edges of the fountain, and she traced her fingertips over their silken petals while examining the sculpture. There was something familiar about these figures, but she couldn't think exactly of what it was. In the dim light of the moon, the women seemed to almost move among the flowing water.

But the most wonderful thing of all was the enormous number of roses. The air was saturated with their perfume, and it was the most amazing thing she'd ever smelled. Sharp tones mixed with the heavy sweetness of Old World flowers. The fountain cleared the air enough so it wasn't overwhelming, just an amazing olfactory experience.

A faint glow on the other side caught her eye, and she wandered over to investigate, curling her toes in the grass and enjoying the faint scent from the crushed blades. On the opposite side of the fountain lay an enormous white blanket and two brass lanterns. There was also a plate of fruit and chocolate as well as a few decadent pastries. Her suddenly empty tummy growled, and she sighed.

"This is amazing. Almost perfect."

"Almost?"

She lowered her lashes and gave him the look that never failed to bring men running. "There is just one more thing that would make this perfect."

He looked amused, but she could sense a sudden tension in him. His eyes grew darker, and he took a step closer, sitting on the edge of the fountain next to her. "What would that be?"

"Could you *please* help me get out of this corset? I'm starving, but I can't eat anything with it on."

He shook his head and motioned her closer. "You're terrible. Turn around."

She did as he asked, then shivered as his fingers stroked down her back to the top of the lacings. "You know, I find latex to be amazing stuff. You're fully covered, but at the same time, it's like you're naked. And curves like yours look amazing in it."

She sighed in relief as he began to loosen the corset, and her lungs filled fully with air for the first time in hours.

Each little tug set her off-balance, and she found herself leaning back into him, her thighs braced on the outside by his firm legs and by the fountain behind her. His movements slowed, and he slid his hands beneath the now loose waist corset, massaging her lower back.

"Better?"

She fought the urge to melt and managed a breathy "Yes" in reply.

He laughed and tugged at the corset. "It will be easier if you shimmy it down instead of unlacing it all the way."

Giving in to a wicked impulse, she pulled the corset down her legs and bent over in an exaggerated slow movement, conscious of Isaac's body cradling hers. She kicked the silver corset off and turned around with a grin that faded at the fierce look on his face.

His nostrils flared, and he closed his eyes. "Lucia, you are playing with fire."

Startled, she took a step back. "I—I'm sorry."

"I don't mind a bit of flirting, and there is no way I can be around you and not be attracted to you, but this is not a good idea."

"Oh, okay." Stung by his rejection, she crossed her arms over her chest in a vain effort to shield her stupid heart. "No big deal. It would be better if we remained strictly platonic while alone."

He opened his eyes a crack. "Well, maybe we could make a tiny exception."

She shook her head and moved away to the blanket, spotting a piece of chocolate that had comfort written on it. "Nope, you're right. I never want to be involved with a man who questions if he should be with me."

The blanket must be filled with down feathers, because when she lay on her back and picked a chocolate off the tray, she sank back into its fluffy comfort. He joined her a moment later, but she ignored him and watched the thin clouds pass by the moon. Three pieces of chocolate later, she was more pissed at herself than at him. He was being a gentleman, trying to do the right thing while she threw herself at him.

He sat up on his elbows and took a slug of the champagne and looked out at the garden. "You know, Sara's husband had these rosebushes brought in from all around the world. One bush from each place they'd visited. The collection of French roses are among the best anywhere."

"That is lovely." She sat up and grabbed the bottle from him, not giving a crap if her stomach pouched out a bit. Curves all over meant curves on bellies as well. Not that half the starving women at this club would know that. She'd seen bare bellies all night taut enough to bounce a quarter off.

Male and female.

The cool alcohol hit her tongue, and she took a long drink, reveling in the bursting of bubbles that tickled her as only champagne could. She broke off and examined the label of the bottle. "Jeez, Louise! We shouldn't be drinking this! This is for super special occasions, like weddings and funerals."

"Or for enjoying on a beautiful summer's night in January." He seemed amused by her shock.

With a laugh she considered this and shook her head. "You're darn right it is." She then took one last slug of the champagne and handed the bottle back to him with a giggle.

He did that weird stare again, then burst out laughing. He looked so hot when he was laughing. Then again he'd probably look hot to her brushing his teeth in the morning. Or doing...things to her. Things she'd never even considered but now couldn't wait to try with the right guy.

"Look, Mr. Jaded, I'm sorry, but to those of us not

living in the top one percent, this is pretty amazing." She picked a peach slice and bit into it with a moan. "Have you tasted this fruit? It is unreal. I haven't had peaches this fresh since the last time I visited my grandma's home down in Mexico."

"Pick one for me and feed it to me with your fingers."

She paused in the act of licking peach juice from her fingers. "Pardon me?"

"You heard me. Your rhapsodizing about the food has made me hungry. And since it is your fault, you will alleviate the hunger you've started."

"Are you sure?"

"That I'm hungry? Yes."

She frowned at him. "You know what I mean. Your 'this is a mistake' speech earlier didn't seem to indicate a hunger of any kind."

He ducked his head and gave her a crooked smile. "I'm reevaluating the rules of our partnership. They now include you feeding me. Do you find those terms acceptable?"

"What do I get out of it?"

"Tomorrow night I'll make you orgasm with one kiss."

She stared at him and started to giggle. "Are you going to slip me some Ecstasy?"

"No, and I will never touch you with my hands on your flesh. The only skin that will touch is our lips, and I promise you that you will orgasm like you never have before. Now, about that fruit?"

She was afraid if she pressed her thighs together, she would come, but damn, she'd have to be a fool to pass up an opportunity like that. Even if they were just business partners, it didn't mean they couldn't both be adults about it. "Yes, sir." She crawled over to the food and put a little slink in her stride. With the cat mask, moving like a feline became fun. While her butt was still in the air, she picked up a slice of peach with her teeth.

She was determined to get a kiss from him tonight to figure out what he intended for her. Lightly sucking on the peach, she unzipped her catsuit until her breasts were about falling out. With a slow arch, she turned and tossed her hair over her shoulder. Isaac gripped the blanket with both fists, and his body seemed to thrum with tension. His big cock certainly appreciated her display. It filled out the front of his slacks, and she almost growled with need.

Good Lord, put a cat face on her, and she turned into some kind of kinky sex beast. She'd like to blame it on the champagne, but since the moment she'd met the man, her body had cried out for her to take him. To be his and to make him hers. It was irrational, stupid even, considering his repeated statements about not wanting a relationship, but she wanted him more than she wanted air. Somehow she should be able to keep her heart out of this, to keep it just physical between them.

His blue eyes blazed as she neared, but he held up his hand. "Take it out of your mouth and put it between your breasts."

Flushing, she hesitated and removed the peach. Keeping her eyes down, she traced the fruit along the side of her neck, the side still tingling from his kiss, and pressed it between her breasts.

"Now, go sit on the edge of the fountain, but don't lose the fruit."

She cocked her head and raised her eyebrows, but he gave her a cool, almost impassive look. It seemed like the more they played the more focused he got. Goodness, what would it be like to have his attention totally on her? What would it feel like to have a man touch her who keyed in to every nuance of her body?

Pressing her arms against the sides of her breasts kept the fruit in place, she zipped up the top a bit more and let go of her breasts. Isaac stood, and some trick of the light hid half his face from her in shadows. "Lie down."

She cleared her throat but complied, stretching out on the wide marble shelf surrounding the fountain and enjoying the cool breeze of the mist. As she stared at the figures from this angle, she started to sit up. "Hey, this statue—"

Her words cut off as he slid one arm behind her back and licked his way down the side of her neck, following the trail of the peach. Lust flamed through her body, and she ached for him. She wanted to taste him, smell him, be his. With a low growl he rasped his tongue over the top of the fruit, and he slowly ate it from the valley between her breasts.

She clutched him to her, unashamed and desperate in her need. His laughter vibrated against her skin as she tried to guide him to a nipple.

With one deft move, he lowered her back to the fountain's wide ledge and pinned her hands above her head. "You don't get to decide what I do, Kitten."

"Okay, seriously, if you don't do something, I'm going to die right here, right now, of unfulfilled lust. I'll haunt you for the rest of your days."

He grinned and shook his head. "No wonder you like Chloe. You're both more than honest when riled."

She closed her eyes and counted to ten. "Isaac, will you please make me come?"

"No."

"You suck."

"I know, Kitten. But I want to take things slow, to savor you. When you rush, you miss all the good stuff." He helped her off the edge of the fountain. "Besides, I promised you an orgasm with just one kiss, and I intend to deliver."

"It had better be the best damned orgasm I've ever

had, or your face is going to be between my legs quicker than you can blink."

He wrapped her hair in his hand and pulled her forward, his lips moving against her ear as he spoke. "Kitten, believe me when I say that doing what I tell you instead of what you think you want will be far more pleasurable than you can imagine."

Her scalp tingled as he released her hair, and she took a step back and sighed. "I'm tired, and I'd like to get some sleep if you aren't going to give me any relief." She fluttered her lashes at him, and he laughed.

"You are oh so dangerous. Come on, Kitten. I have blankets in the limo, and you can sleep on my shoulder on the way back." He pulled her into his arms and hugged her, his warmth spreading through her and turning her bones to mush.

"I'm not tired."

"I know."

"Well, maybe I'm a little sleepy." She yawned and moved out of his arms, heading for the elevator. "FYI, I snore, but if you wake me up fast, I wake up violent."

He shook his head. "You are one unique woman."

"Damn skippy."

Chapter Six

Isaac tried to pay attention to the droning lecture his twin sister, Gloria, was giving him about their West Coast headquarters, but he couldn't focus on anything but thoughts of Lucia. The way her body looked with that catsuit painted on it. How soft her hair felt wrapped around his fist and how easily she gave in to his desires. But could she really handle how dark his passions ran? Could she truly give herself to him?

That annoyed tone in Gloria's voice broke through his thoughts. "And that's why I'm going to ride an elephant in South Africa for the next two weeks."

He laced his hands behind his head and leaned back in his chair. "Excellent. Maybe that ride will finally dislodge the stick up your ass."

Her blue eyes much like his narrowed, and she stalked over to his desk and picked up his letter opener that could be mistaken for a dagger and pointed it at his neck. "It's actually a monkey up my ass, thank you, and I'll have you know he and I are quite fond of each other." Then she laughed and set the letter opener back down. "So what has you so preoccupied? I know these reports are dull, but I could have been up there giving a speech about snails for all the attention you paid."

"It's nothing." He sat up and opened the file containing

the figures for last month's orange shipments out of California. "How are things going with that new distributor?"

She shook her head and tapped her long pink nail on the surface of his desk. "No, it's more than that. I know that evasive look you get when you're not telling me something. Fess up, or I'll set my spies on you."

Isaac sighed and rested his face in his hands. She wasn't joking. If she felt he was hiding something important, she might try to bribe his staff. The last thing he needed was his sister offending his workforce. The term *boundaries* and Gloria didn't mix.

"I'm thinking about the Valentine's Day party at Wicked."

She made a face. "I don't want to hear about your freaky sex club."

He snorted. "This from the woman who stood in a prostitute's window for an hour in her underwear in Amsterdam."

"It was a dare! And aren't you trying to get on their board of members or something? I remember you prattling about it a few weeks ago."

"Yes, and this party is key to that."

"So? Throw a party. Big deal. It's not like you have no idea what to do. Hire the right people and have it done." Something must have shown on his face, so she leaned closer. "Ooh, there it is. The secret."

"She's just the event planner." He winced at the gleam in his sister's eye. A sudden protective instinct raised its head, and his voice came out a bit harsher than he intended. "She is a good, hardworking, normal person, Gloria. Leave her alone."

With a satisfied smirk Gloria swept her dark hair back. "You like her."

"Perhaps. But it doesn't really matter. You know I'm not into relationships, and this girl is the marrying type."

Gloria rubbed her thumb on her wedding band. "Isaac, not every relationship ends badly."

"One divorce is enough for me. I don't want to go down that road again, ever."

She sighed and moved around the desk to his side, ruffling his hair. "So you had a bad first marriage. You were young, stupid, and arrogant. In short you were a typical teenager. Let me let you in on a little secret. When you get married at eighteen, you really don't know shit about shit. In this case, you got manipulated by a cheating, evil skank who wanted your money more than you. You've got to let it go, honey."

"You'd feel different if it happened to you, if Mike had an affair." She flinched, and he felt guilty for hurting her. "Look, I'm sorry." She still looked wounded, so he gave in and told her the truth. "I'm on edge because I have a date with her tonight, and I'm a little stressed about it."

"That is so cute!"

He stiffened and glared at her. "What?"

"You're nervous about a date because she actually means something to you."

He wanted to deny it, but lying to his twin wasn't easy. "Maybe." He was also unsure about his self-control around Lucia. She brought out the beast in him without even trying. He planned on not giving in to his desires and making it all about her pleasure. That way he would keep himself out of it and just focus on her. Yeah, once this party was over, he'd be able to walk away without any strings attached, leaving her with good memories and a better understanding of herself. Some lucky Dom would snatch her up, and Isaac would continue on with his life, alone and once again in complete control of his life and emotions. Shit, even he had to admit that made him sound like a cold fucking bastard.

Lucia deserved better than what he could give her.

"I just don't want to hurt her."

"Then don't. Give it a chance. If something happens, awesome. If not, well, isn't that what you want as well? It sounds like a win-win situation."

"If only it were that easy." His cell phone vibrated on the corner of the desk, and he glanced at the incoming call. It was from Lucia. "Hold on one sec."

Moving a little too quickly to be casual, he picked up the phone and answered the call. "Hello, Lucia."

"Hi, Isaac. I'm still at Laurel's dress shop. This place is amazing! I mean, seriously, it's like stepping into the costume warehouse of a major Hollywood studio. She said that she is going to dress me for tonight and wants to do my hair and all of that. Like I'm her Latina dress-up doll."

He heard Laurel laughing in the background. "Tell her I don't share my toys."

"I'm not repeating that. Oh, and can you bring some dinner with you?" Laurel said something in the background, and Lucia laughed. "She said you need to wear your leathers. Okay, I have to go. I'll see you in a few hours."

"See you then." He hung up and turned to find his sister smirking at him. "What?"

"You should have seen your smile when you answered that call. Was that her?"

"I have some work I need to take care of. Why don't you go to the spa, my treat?"

She laughed and gathered up her things. "Fine, fine, I'll go. But I want you to know you can call me if you get nervous. And I would like to meet her at some point. You know, if she lasts longer than two weeks."

He glared at her as she left. Gloria made it sound so

easy, but it wasn't. Not only did he not want to get hurt again, but he didn't want to hurt anyone else. His ex had done a number on him in the brief year they'd been married, and it had taken him a long time to heal. Now that he finally felt whole and happy with his life, he didn't want to complicate things. And Lucia would definitely complicate them.

Yep, he needed to stay as far away from Lucia as he could.

That goal lasted him all of about three seconds before he picked up the phone and ordered dinner for the three of them. His refusal to fall in love also didn't stop him from leaving work early and going to his house and changing into his jeans and a T-shirt. He even grabbed the bag hanging in the closet containing his leathers, imagining her pleased reaction at seeing him fully in his role as her Master. And it didn't stop the anticipation at seeing her again that burned through him during the drive to Laurel's business.

—*—

Two hours later he smiled at Laurel as she held the door open for him. "Oh God, you brought us BLT Steaks! Did you get me the aged New York Strip?"

"Of course." He stepped into the cavernous first level of a big building with its racks and racks of clothing. Laurel was married to one of the top producers on Broadway and was also a professional seamstress. She not only supplied costumes for movies and theater productions all over the world, but she also made fetish clothing for select friends. Usually she had a small army of seamstresses working beneath her, but today they were alone in the enormous space.

"Where's Lucia?"

"She's getting back into her street clothes." His disappointment must have shown, because she laughed.

"She'll be here soon."

"Where do you want this?"

"Follow me."

She led him through a maze of costumes hanging in clear plastic and paused when they reached a section containing what looked like fur coats. "This Lucia, she isn't like the girls you usually slut around with."

"I don't think that's any of your business, and I don't slut around with anyone."

"It is my business because I like her, and she *really* likes you."

"I don—wait, she likes me? She told you that?" He sighed and closed his eyes. "Fuck, I sound like an idiot."

"Men often sound like idiots. It's perfectly normal." She started walking again but kept her voice low. "She had a bunch of questions about the lifestyle for me today but swore me to secrecy about them. I can tell you that you should be ready to negotiate with her before you do anything, likes and dislikes, safe words, and all of that fun stuff."

He wanted to throttle Laurel, but his hands were full of food bags. "What have you done?"

"Don't worry. It was mostly stuff pertaining to the Valentine's Day party. You know, the one Morgana always does."

"Used to do." He shrugged. "It's not like Morgana needed the work. She's loaded, and I'm tired of her dark and creepy-themed parties."

"Well, don't leave Lucia alone around her. From what I've heard she is having quite a tiff about it, and you know how blunt she can be."

"If she does one thing to make Lucia upset, I'll get her booted out of Wicked faster than she can blink."

"Easy there, tiger."

They rounded the corner and came to a big circular white table covered with sewing stuff. Laurel moved a stack of fabric and drawings onto the counter beneath the cabinets and shelves along the back wall. She pulled out a stack of mismatched plates and cups while he set the meal next to her. She paused and arched a brow. "That's a lot of food. Are we having company?"

He tried to ignore the heat burning his cheeks and focused on the packages. "I didn't know what Lucia would like."

"So you got her one of everything?"

"Not everything. Just chicken, steak, and fish."

Laurel grinned but wisely didn't say anything, and they finished setting up in silence. As he was filling their glasses with water, the sound of feet coming down the stairs made him look up. Lucia paused near the bottom step and smiled. His heart stuttered, and his cock twitched. Dressed in a pair of jeans and a pink T-shirt, she looked good enough to eat. The sexy way her long hair swung to her hips made him yearn to bury his hands in it as she sucked him.

She tilted her head and gave him a smile. "Hi. Take off your jacket and stay awhile."

Suddenly all of his anxiety went away, replaced by happiness. He grinned and set the glass down. "Suppose I could take my jacket off." He removed the black wool trench coat and slung it back over the chair.

"Where are your leather pants?"

"I'm not going to eat in them. You wouldn't find me so hot if they smelled like steak."

She finished coming down the stairs while Laurel chuckled. "I don't know. It might be tasty."

Minx. He stared at her swaying backside as she passed him and took a seat at the table. With effort he forced himself to keep it light and easy, smiling at Lucia as if he didn't want to throw her down on the table and fuck the hell out of her.

He managed to control himself, and they had a nice dinner together. Lucia laughed at the variety of meals available. She ended up going with the chicken. The moan of pleasure she made at the first bite tightened his balls. He thought that jerking off twice in the shower would have made it easier to control libido, but he found himself as aroused as ever. Everything about Lucia captivated him, and he tried to keep from staring at her.

He watched her eat, the way her full lips parted for the fork, how her silken throat moved when she swallowed. When her tongue darted out to catch a bit of sauce from the corner of her mouth, he forgot to swallow, and when she asked for a bit of his steak and he fed her, the need to kiss her almost overwhelmed him. But it was her quick wit and humor that enchanted him, the way the world came to life when she was around. Smart, ambitious, kind, and beautiful, she was the total package. He knew he was playing with fire, that his feelings for her were getting harder to deny, but like a starving man standing before a banquet, he couldn't tear himself away.

Finally Laurel stood up and tossed her napkin on the table. "Do you mind cleaning up while I get her ready?"

Lucia stood as well and rubbed her belly. "Great. Stuff me full of food, then put me in that outfit."

The women laughed and headed upstairs while Isaac slipped into one of the dressing rooms. He quickly changed into his leather pants and black T-shirt, deciding on wearing the leather vest another time. He went back out to the kitchen area and cleaned up their mess. He'd finished drying the last dish when the sound of whispering women's voices and giggles came from the stairs.

He moved to the table and leaned against it, trying to

appear like he hadn't been eagerly waiting for her. He caught a glimpse of gold jewelry and sparkles adorning her leg before the rest of her appeared and he forgot to breathe. Intense emotions and lust flooded him, and he tried to control his expression, to not let her know how much her beauty affected him.

In his experience once a woman knew he'd fallen for her, she'd then use her beauty and his desire against him. His ex-wife certainly had, and although Lucia was nothing like her, he still couldn't help trying to hide the strength of his attraction from her. A small, vulnerable part of his soul was afraid of what she would do if she knew how much power she had over him. If Lucia asked for the sun, he'd burn himself up trying to get it for her. And now, standing before him like every erotic fantasy come to life was a woman who personified beauty. He'd move mountains and drain seas for the honor of her company. His mind spun, torn between his body's craving for the beautiful woman before him and his need to protect his heart. Then she smiled at him, and there was such shy pleasure in her eyes that he couldn't help but give her his honest reaction. He let the heat, the ball-tightening need burning him from the inside out show in his eyes, and her breath came out in a soft gasp as her gaze went dark and liquid.

She wore what could only be described as an intricate piece of gold and diamond body jewelry that covered her from head to toe but left most of her flesh deliciously bare. A bikini top covered her breasts, and a tiny scrap of fabric shielded her pussy from his ravenous view. On her arms and legs she had glittering chains wound about in an appealing way. Her feet were bare, and the chains going down her legs attached to gold rings on her toes.

He tore his gaze from her body and watched her face as she took the last few steps. Her hair lung loose down her back like a cloak. A bright blush lit her cheeks, and she clasped her hands together over her midriff, her fluttering fingers trying to hide the round curve of her belly that he found so fucking hot. How Lucia couldn't recognize her own beauty surprised him. If she'd been one of the socialites he'd grown up with, she would have been winding him around her little finger right now with coquettish looks and suggestive comments. Lucia's honest and unsure response enchanted him. The Dom part of him wanted to hold her, to let her know that he was pleased with her, that her efforts to look beautiful for him were the greatest gift she could give him. The old wounds that his ex had left on his heart ached, and he tried to pull back emotionally.

She must have noticed his efforts to distance himself, because her gaze dropped to the floor. Her voice came out soft and hesitant as she asked, "Do you like it?"

Dammit, he'd made her feel unsure about herself all because of his fucked-up head. While he couldn't be everything she deserved, he could at least be her Master. That part of him wasn't conflicted. His dominant side knew exactly what she needed and strove to fulfill her every desire. She'd trusted him to be her Master, however temporarily, and he wasn't going to fuck that up. Unable to stop himself, he took her hands in his, then pulled them away from her body, putting the feelings he couldn't speak into his tone. "You are the most exquisite thing I've ever seen."

She flushed and looked down at herself. "I feel like Jabba the Hutt's slave girl from a porn version of *Star Wars*."

His laughter burst from him, and he grabbed her in a hug, pressing all that softness up against himself. It was torture to not ravish her right here. "*My* slave girl."

Laurel came down the stairs with a swath of gold fabric. "Hey, get your hands off her. I want her to look good when you arrive at the club. So that means no messy, sweaty encounters in the limo."

He pulled himself together and released Lucia. The affection that he couldn't show her as a boyfriend he could show her as a Dom. It was expected, a part of the intricate dance of dominance and submission that Laurel knew so well. Hopefully she wouldn't notice that this time, he actually did feel a proprietary hold over his submissive that went way beyond a casual BDSM physical relationship. "Actually, I drove tonight, so while I'd love to do terrible things to the lovely Lucia, I'm afraid I must attend to her safety first and get her there in one piece."

With a gentle tug Laurel tried to pull Lucia from his arms, but Lucia held on to him until Laurel gave a disgruntled snort and pulled harder. "Here, put this robe on."

The glittering fabric swirled around Lucia and completely covered her, but it was semitransparent. He caught glimpses of sparkle and flash through the cloth, and it made him wonder what she looked like under there, even though he already knew.

Lucia fingered the robe. "Thank God. I was praying you weren't going to make me walk around in there dressed only in that bikini."

"I don't share," Isaac said and brushed back a stray wisp of hair from her cheek. He moved behind her and pulled the medallion with the word *mine* out of his pocket. "Lift your hair." She complied, and some urge drove him to kiss the back of her neck before tying it on, breathing in her warm vanilla scent. His lips brushed her skin, and she stilled, then let out a soft sigh when he licked the smooth spot where her neck met her shoulder. She leaned back against him, tilting her head and encouraging more.

Her trust in him was evident in her every action, and he relished it even as he cursed himself for liking it. Yes, trust between a Master and a submissive was essential in any BDSM relationship, even just a physical one, but he cared more about the soft smile curving her lips when she leaned her head back on his chest than any evidence of her body's arousal. Making her happy made him happy, and he tried to ignore the insidious voice inside him that warned he was only going to get hurt. No, he wouldn't get hurt, because he was doing what any Master would do for his submissive. Before he'd only picked women who needed his physical dominance, but Lucia was different. Her submission was total, not just her body but her mind and soul.

If he had a soul, he'd leave her alone, but he just couldn't.

Trying to gather his wits, he took his jacket and draped it over Lucia's shoulders. "The car has heated seats, so you should warm up pretty quick."

She grinned up at him and gave a mock shiver. "Yeah, I don't think I want cold metal pressing on my girly bits."

"Indeed." His voice came out strangled as he imagined warming those delectable bits with his mouth. He escorted Lucia from of the building with Laurel's laughter trailing after them.

When they reached the doorway, Lucia squeaked and jumped back. "Shoot, I totally forgot my feet are bare."

He laughed and scooped her up, loving the warm feel of her against his chest, enjoying the way her long hair cascaded over his arm, and how she clung to him.

"What are you doing? Put me down before you drop me."

He ignored her tirade and used his shoulder to open the door, making sure she was still covered by the jacket. "Stop squirming, or I will drop you."

Her wiggles stopped, and she shivered. "Okay, well, if you insist, then put a move on it. I'm freezing."

Then she burrowed into him like a cat, and he wanted

to stroke her until she purred. He chuckled at the mental image of a purring Lucia sleeping at his feet, and she gave him a grumpy look. "I don't even want to know what your perverted mind was thinking."

She peeked out of his jacket at his car. "Wow. Nice shiny black spaceship."

Laughing, he brushed his lips over her hair. "It's a concept SUV that isn't in production in the States yet."

"My brother would die just to breathe on it." She shivered. "I personally don't care what we drive in as long as it's warm."

With a bit of maneuvering, he got the door to the SUV open and slid her onto the seat. Her pout disappeared as she sighed. "Ooh, it's warm in here."

He shut the door with a grin that faded as he wondered how he'd ever let her go.

CHAPTER SEVEN

Lucia looked around the now dark interior of the SUV and mentally whistled. Extremely comfortable cream and tan seats molded against her body. She'd never ridden in a car that felt like she was sitting in an easy chair. It was also incredibly silent inside, enough so the only sound she heard was the very faint strains of music coming from the radio and their breathing. She'd enjoyed the silence while they'd been on the freeway, using the time to gather her thoughts, but as they took an exit off the highway, she started to get restless.

Her gaze went to the dashboard that was classic and thoroughly modern. There were all kinds of instruments, but she didn't see one button or dial. Curious, she leaned forward and studied the car's stereo.

"What are you doing?" Isaac asked, his deep voice moving over her body like melted chocolate.

Madre de Dios, how did he manage to make everything sensual, even just a simple question? It was as if he had some type of magic, a spell specially attuned to drive her wild. She wanted him to keep talking, to make her body hum with pleasure as his voice vibrated through her blood and straight to her clit. Hell, that man could read the phone book, and she'd be wet and ready before he finished the first row of names.

"I'm trying to figure out how to turn up the volume."

"Here." He switched his hands on the steering wheel and enveloped hers in his heat. His skin felt so warm, and she noted the slight roughness of his fingertips. Using the tip of her finger, he showed her how to operate the volume on the touch-screen display.

A hard, pounding beat came from the speakers, and she laughed in delight. Bass shook her body from the inside out; she was glad they were on the freeway, or this car would have caused noise complaints.

He turned it down to a manageable level and grinned. "What can I say? I like my Nine Inch Nails."

She thumped back into the seat and sighed. "I have got to get me one of these." She looked over at him to judge his reactions. "So, I have something to ask you."

His jaw tensed, but then he blew out a breath. "What's up?"

"Do the people at the club like to dress up in costumes for your parties? I mean, with all the outrageous outfits I saw last night and this galactic slave-girl getup I'm wearing, I'm wondering if the members would enjoy a party they could dress up for. I have a drawing of what I was thinking of in my bag, which is back at Laurel's place." She sighed and smacked her forehead. "Honest to goodness. Usually I'm much more organized than this. It's just that you make me nervous."

"I make you nervous?"

She bit her wayward tongue and reluctantly nodded. "Not like in a bad *oh my God he wants to eat my liver with fava beans* way. More like...I don't know...like butterflies in my stomach or something."

"Really." The smug smile that curved his lips made her want to smack him.

"I think I might be allergic to you."

He laughed and pulled off the freeway onto a side road. "I'll try not to shed or slobber on you."

"So, back to my original question, what do you think?"

He ran his tongue over his bottom lip and glanced at her. "I think a costume party would be a big hit. But please don't make it all dark and dreary. Our last event planner, Lady Morgana, had a thing for vampires, so every event she did felt like an emo prom. The board at Wicked finally got tired of it, and when I found out they were looking for someone else to host the party, I volunteered. All of the board members of Wicked are actively involved in the day-to-day running of the club. They set the tone for Wicked, and over the years the club has gone through many incarnations…some good and some not so good. I love Wicked, not only for the pleasures it offers, but because of the people. I know you haven't really interacted with anyone yet, but for the most part, the people that belong to Wicked are some of the best you'll ever meet. I want Wicked to continue to be a place that my friends and I can meet to not only indulge in our passions, but also to relax and be among friends."

He glanced over at her and grinned. "Sorry for the lecture, but I want you to know why this is so important to me. It's not just about getting on the board for the privileges and power that comes with that position. While I certainly enjoy the benefits, I really want to be on it so I can prevent the assholes and bitches of the world from turning Wicked into just another place where people fuck. Am I making any sense? I feel like I'm babbling."

"No, no, I totally understand." She turned to face him as much as she could in her seat. "You want to keep the magic alive. There is like…a feeling to Wicked, like when you first step inside you're parting the veil of reality and entering an entirely different world."

He smiled and nodded. "In a way, yeah."

"Well, I'll do my absolute best to help you throw the best damned Valentine's Day party that club has ever seen."

"Please tell me you don't have the urge to make a Dracula-themed Valentine's Day."

"God, no. Besides, that's too cliché. I want to do something different, something they will remember."

"What do you have in mind?"

"Well, you know how Wicked is all secret hush-hush because BDSM is considered morally questionable by society in general? How it's kind of a forbidden type of love? I was thinking we do a play off of that."

"Sounds like an interesting concept. How are you going to execute it?"

"I was thinking of a speakeasy Valentine's Day party. We'll transform one of the ballrooms into an illicit bar from the 1920s. Men can be gangsters, cops, whatever they want from that time period, and for the women they have the fabulous flappers as inspiration. Instead of highlighting how liquor was illegal, we'll do it showcasing BDSM as the forbidden pleasure of choice. You know, have gaming tables with some kind of BDSM-themed card games or a bar where you can order a submissive to flog instead of a drink. I'd need your help in figuring all of that stuff out, but just think of how amazing we could make this."

In her mind visions of designs and floral creations mixed with the number of workers they would need. Which led to her thinking about where they would find white peonies this time of year. If they preordered now, could she find some of those roses that were so deep red they almost looked black? She needed to find out who to talk to in order to get access to Wicked during the day when no members were around so she could start getting measurements. She also needed to get together with whoever was in charge of alcohol and see who they ordered from so she could use the same company, and then contact the company to find out what kind of liquor and wine they sold the most of—

"Lucia," Isaac said in a loud, teasing voice. "Earth to Lucia, are you there?"

"Oh, sorry. I was thinking about how much we have to get done. So many people to contact, and I need to—"

"Lucia, it is going to be okay. You aren't doing this alone. I'm here to help you. Between the two of us, we can get anything done that needs to be done. Now, deep breath in." He looked expectantly at her as they turned down a tree-lined street flanked with enormous homes set back from the road.

She did as he said and glanced around curiously. On the limo ride up she hadn't paid much attention to anything but Isaac. Not that the same thing wasn't happening right now, but she wanted to at least know what the exterior of Wicked looked like.

"Open the glove box. Your mask is in there. Might want to put it on before we arrive."

She nodded, then flipped open the glove box and pulled out a white silk case. "This isn't my mask. It was in a black case."

He grinned, and she couldn't help but smile back. "I had masks made in a variety of colors for you. Laurel told me which one to bring."

She glanced at him but couldn't read anything in his gaze. It must have cost a fortune to get so many masks so quickly. Did that mean that he liked her, or that money was not an issue with him so he never thought about what things cost? She'd like to believe the former, but her practical side insisted she not let him dazzle her with wealth and blind her to his faults. Lord knew she'd seen it happen often enough with her friends. But it wasn't like she was going to keep any of this stuff. After they were done, she'd either pay him for the cost of the clothes or return them. Hopefully she could return them, because she was pretty sure it would take half of what she earned to reimburse Isaac.

Brushing away those thoughts, she tried to focus on the moment. Soft silk rubbed against her fingertips as she opened the box to reveal a golden mask that had a definite feline feel to it. She noticed something still gleaming in the box and brought out a pair of golden cat ears attached to a headband that matched her dark hair color.

"Seriously?"

He gave her a warm look, and the faint lines around his mouth deepened. "Oh yes."

"I'll look silly!"

"No, you won't. Did you know that yesterday the gentleman who makes my masks had a rush on new orders for cat-type masks? Now, there may be a bunch of women there tonight in some type of cat getup, but none of them are like you, my kitten."

"Ha, more like a killer lioness." She bared her teeth at him and snarled. "Grrr."

"Pathetic."

"Oh yeah? Let me hear your roar."

"The only time you'll get to hear my roar is when I've fucked you into a state of bliss and I spill myself deep inside your tight body."

"Oh," she said in a faint voice and stared at him. "You think you're gonna get lucky tonight, don't you?"

"No." His features tightened, and his eyelids grew heavy. "Tonight is all about your pleasure."

He pulled up a winding driveway before reaching a massive and elaborately carved wrought-iron gate. It was illuminated by great cut-glass lanterns on either side and would have looked perfect guarding the entrance to a castle. She noticed the thick concrete pillars thrusting up and blocking the drive beyond the gate and modified her imaginings from a delicate fairy castle to an imposing and impressive fortress.

Even though they hadn't even entered the property yet, a delicious shiver went through her. Passing through these gates was like passing through a portal to another world. A fantasy place where any pleasure that could be bought was and the only thing limiting the wonders within was the owner's imagination. After experiencing the garden in the sky, she didn't know what could possibly top it. A flush of embarrassment heated her cheeks at the silly, romantic turn her thoughts had taken, but never in her life would she have imagined not only that places like this existed, but that she'd be eagerly waiting to enter with a handsome and wicked prince.

Isaac pulled up and tapped a code into a gate box. A moment later a disembodied female voice spoke from the box. "Good evening, Mr. O'Keefe. You are expected."

Before them the heavy black iron bars opened, and the concrete barriers beyond lowered. Isaac drove through, following a driveway lit with exquisite wrought-iron lanterns. Bare tree branches curved over the drive, and they probably went another quarter mile before pulling within sight of the club.

It was all she had imagined and more.

Lights blazed from every window of the four-story mansion, illuminating the pale stone exterior with their golden glow and revealing columned porches, balconies, and vast windows.

He went around the main parking area with its covered entrance, waving at the valet, before pulling up behind the mansion next to what looked like a steel black door with security cameras pointed at it. Every breath he took seemed to burn her skin, and when he turned off the car and picked the cat mask up from the seat, she actually trembled.

She was glad she didn't have to face a crowd. Yesterday she'd been too excited to really think about who she was and who they were. Stroking her fingers over the mask, she reminded herself that no matter how rich and famous someone was, she was on the arm of one of the most eligible bachelors in the world. A man who had promised to make her orgasm with just a kiss.

The man sitting next to her, making her body buzz with an erotic charge caused by his look.

The dome light of the car dimmed to a low golden glow, which seemed bright. Her breath caught in her throat as their gazes met, and she was captured by him as surely as a snake by its charmer. A faint hint of stubble darkened his chin, and her fingers itched to touch him, to brush her thumbs over the harsh angles of his jaw, to press her lips to his, and surrender to his every demand.

Earlier today when she'd been talking to Laurel about BDSM, she'd been imagining what Isaac would do to her tonight. It had left her in an almost constant state of arousal. Now the simmering craving for his touch roared back to life, blanketing her mind with feelings and chasing away her thoughts. With one look from him, he'd managed to reduce her to a throbbing puddle of hormones.

The first brush of his fingertips smoothing the hair away from her face had her closing her eyes and leaning into his stroke. Her whole body strained toward him, needing him, wanting to be his. She yearned for the bond that Laurel had described, the complete trust between a Master and his submissive. The ability to let go, to fly, and know that he would be there to catch her. Her mind tried to chide her about being silly and impulsive, but even her own thoughts had no power over her when she was the focus of Isaac's full attention. Her body hummed with the electricity that arched between them.

He cupped her face and smoothed the mask on with his free hand. Each caress filled her with warmth, joy, and desire. She couldn't think of a time when a man had touched her so tenderly yet firmly. With the mask in place, he pulled back and watched her in the dim light with burning hunger.

"Before we leave this car tonight, I want to get a few things clear between us, Kitten."

She nodded and tried to rein in her hormones. Being reduced to this drooling state around him had become embarrassingly frequent. Her discussion with Laurel came to mind, and she mentally steadied herself. She wanted Isaac to know that she'd been paying attention, that she really had been researching the lifestyle, and not just the sex parts. Looking away helped, so she stared out the windshield toward the hulking stone mass that was Wicked. Just the sight of the building helped her focus and regain control because it represented everything she'd worked so hard for. She glanced back over at Isaac and took a deep breath.

"Yes, I—uh, that is we need to negotiate first." His lips twitched, and she swore he looked amused, but she chose to ignore it. "Okay, my no-way-in-hell list. No burning, branding, bleeding, cutting, choking, extreme bondage, extreme shibari, spitting, humiliation, or face slapping. Also no degradation or calling me names. And no potty stuff. Yuck."

"Quite a list, but I happen to agree with you on all of those things. But you said extreme bondage and extreme shibari, correct? Mild bondage interests you?"

She nodded and swallowed hard at some of the erotic images that came to mind.

He smiled like a cat that had gotten the canary. "Agreed."

"And my safe word is penicillin."

"Penicillin?"

"Yeah, I'm allergic to it, and Laurel said to pick a word we never would really use in sex play...unless one of us was like a doctor or something." She cleared her throat at the erotic mental images that statement brought and smiled. "And that's about it, right? I didn't, like, miss a step or anything, did I?"

Cripes, she felt like such a goober. She hadn't been this awkward around a guy since junior high. To make it worse, she really wanted to impress him, to come off as sophisticated as he was. Laurel had said that the initial negotiation was one of the most important parts of BDSM. She'd said that Lucia needed to be totally honest with Isaac and let him know what she needed from him. Just because he was a Master didn't mean he was a mind reader, but she didn't really like how vulnerable it made her feel. Then again, if she didn't trust him enough to talk to him, she really shouldn't be doing anything with him in the first place.

"You did forget to tell me your list of what you liked, but I'd rather find that out for myself." He paused and lifted his hand, gently stroking along the side of her neck with the tip of his finger. "You can trust me."

When he said that, she was reminded of all the guys she'd dated who'd ever said those words. Usually anytime a man said that, it was because he was about to screw her, and not in a good way. She looked into his eyes, straining to judge his sincerity in the dim light. He seemed like he meant it, but she didn't know if that was because he was speaking the truth or her heart was once again seeing things that weren't there.

Trying to play off how much he affected her, she snorted and leaned back. "I've heard that one before."

"I don't lie. In fact, I may be painfully and callously honest, but I don't lie." He sighed and pulled back. "I also don't want you to confuse my instructing you in BDSM as a relationship. While I do care about you, I'll never be in a committed emotional relationship with anyone."

His words stung and almost brought tears to her eyes. Then again, he didn't tell her that to be mean but rather to give her a reality check. He watched her, a weary tilt to his head as if he expected her to freak out. Pretending to be an urbane woman used to such statements, she smiled. "Good, then we are in an agreement. You can date other people, and so can I."

His brow furrowed. "I don't share."

"Well, what a coincidence, neither do I."

He glared at her, and she glared at him until he closed his eyes and shook his head. "Fine, let's say this. Neither of us will have sexual interactions with others while you're in training with me. I believe that is fair. But if you agree, that means for these next few weeks you are my submissive in truth, Kitten." His gaze raked her from head to toe. "All of you, every single inch of your silky golden skin, is mine to play with, mine to pleasure, mine to devour."

Holy crap, she thought she just had an orgasm.

No, she wouldn't be ruled by her hormones. Rallying her remaining brain cells, she considered his words. This was important. Laurel had said the negotiation stage was one of the most significant things to go over before she did a scene with anyone. The thoughts of all the things she didn't want to do came to mind, chief among them being her total distaste for kissing ass and scraping to anyone in public. No matter how hot he was, her pride wouldn't allow it.

"Okay. But outside in the real world, I don't have to bow down or stuff like that to you, do I?"

"No, I'm not into relationships where the Dom and sub are always in their respective roles. Takes too much energy, and I don't want that much control or responsibility over anyone. I want a woman who I can respect that submits to me out of her own free will and desires to please me. Someone I can talk with and expect to have an opinion and mind of her own but who still wants to serve me."

She didn't know about a desire to serve, but she definitely wanted to see what he had to offer. Talking about what was going to happen, before it happened was strangely freeing. She didn't have to worry about tiptoeing around sensitive subjects, and the ability to speak her mind was a relief. No wonder this BDSM stuff appealed to people. If nothing else, it opened up communication, something a lot of her relationships had been sorely lacking.

"We're still equal partners about the party planning, correct? You won't do any of that 'We're doing it my way because I'm a Dom' stuff, right?"

He grinned. "While the thought is tempting, no. Our business is somewhat separate from our pleasure. But once we are at the club or in a private BDSM situation, I expect you to trust me to take care of you."

"That doesn't sound so bad."

She took a deep breath and considered him. Her body flooded with adrenaline as she carefully searched his features. She didn't want this to just be a one-sided thing. His pleasure was important to her. She wanted him to be as aroused as she was. The idea of being the only one getting off just struck her as cold, clinical. He needed to open up to her as well, and even if it embarrassed the hell out of her, she had to ask him in as frank of a manner as she could what he desired.

"What do you want me to do? I mean, what can I do to be a good submissive?"

"Let go of the reins for a while and let me lead." Leaning closer, he grabbed a fistful of her hair and groaned. "Oh, and I love your hair. Never cut it."

She blinked at him, trying to formulate enough

thoughts to tell him to piss off, that she'd wear her hair however she wanted, but he jerked her head back and exposed her neck to his mouth and his teeth. He bit her, then laved the sore spot with his tongue, creating an amazing blend of hurt and pleasure. It certainly sent her body into overdrive, and she clutched at his shoulders, urging him on.

He broke her hold and bit his lower lip. She tried to kiss him, but he held her back and smiled. "Now, put your ears on."

"But—" She shut her mouth at his dark look and sighed. Fine, they were kinda cute anyway. She wrinkled her nose at him but complied, fixing her hair in the dim illumination from the vanity light attached to the visor. As she put the visor up, the black door to Wicked opened, and a big ruddy-skinned man in a charcoal suit appeared. He filled the doorway with his girth and motioned to them.

"Harvey is here to let us in through the Florentines' private entrance. Now, once we get inside, I'm going to blindfold you."

"What? Why?"

He left the car without answering and came over to her side. He opened the door, then lifted her out. Cradling her against him, he carried her through the chilly air. It was too cold to do anything but burrow against him and silently urge him to walk faster. The moment they were inside the dark wood foyer, he set her down and helped her out of his jacket. The security guard gave a low whistle as her costume came into view, and she was ever so glad she wore the mask. At least no one knew it was her acting like such a wanton woman.

Isaac placed a hand on her back in a proprietary manner and took a slight step forward. "Lovely, isn't she?"

The guard nodded and gave her a wink. "I can see why you want to keep her away from the rest of the club. The single Doms would be on her like bees to honey."

Isaac gave a fierce grin and fingered the medallion around her neck. "No, this one is mine. I'm keeping her."

Harvey's jaw dropped, and he looked harder at her. "Really? I mean I can see why…but wow. I think there were a few betting pools on how long it would take you to find the right one." He cleared his throat as his face filled with a flush.

Confused, she looked up to Isaac, but he shook his head. "Later." He turned to Harvey and said in a chilly voice, "You have the green room ready for us?"

The other man gave Isaac an apologetic look. "Of course." He walked over to one of the wooden panels in the wall and revealed a secret access. Beyond it a small wrought-iron staircase curved upwards into darkness. "Have a good night."

Isaac nodded and pulled a black silk scarf out of his pocket. Turning to her, he smiled and ran his thumb over her lower lip, warming her from the inside out. His wicked grin was the last thing she saw before he slipped the cool cloth over her face. She could still almost see her feet if she tilted her head at the right angle, but he caught her and pulled her into his strong arms. "Kitten, I want you to promise me you'll keep your eyes closed behind the blindfold. I want you to get the full effect of the room, and to do that it's best to reveal it to you from the inside."

She pouted and looked in the direction of his voice. "Fine. I promise not to look."

"And I'll trust your word."

Irritated, she muttered something uncomplimentary about his dick in French, and he pinched her bottom, hard enough to make her shriek. "I'll thank you not to compare my dick to a small carrot."

"Umm." She flushed and stumbled when he moved

away. "I'm sorry."

"Not yet, but you will be." While the words were intimidating, his tone was nothing but sensual.

He took her hand and grasped her elbow, his touch helping her navigate the steps. It took an extreme amount of willpower on her part not to peek, to let him guide her when a wrong step could mean both of them tumbling back down. The metal was cool beneath her feet, so she knew they'd made the transition to a new area when soft carpet tickled her toes. She could faintly hear falling water. The sound became louder as Isaac led her forward.

"Can I look?"

"Not yet." He stopped her and pulled her into his arms with her back to his chest. "You seemed to like the fountain, so I thought you might enjoy this."

The silk whispered off her skin, and she blinked, becoming accustomed to the low, almost blue lighting. Right now she was looking at a wooden door that didn't seem too impressive; then Isaac turned them both slowly to the right and tilted her head up. Her breath caught in her throat.

She didn't think anything could top the garden, but she'd been wrong.

A massive stone circle seemed to float over their heads. It wasn't polished smooth, more like raw rock found in a cavern. Somewhere even higher above them, there must be an open pipe, because water poured down the sides of the rock in constant waterfalls. Also descending from the enormous circular ceiling were white, green, and pale pink orchids. As her gaze traveled down to the floor, she noticed they were on an ultramodern island. The carpeting was the same color as the rocks and felt like velvet under her feet. A couch made of white fur faced the room, and a variety of white cushions were scattered on the ground near it.

Isaac turned them farther, and she saw a large white

X suspended from the ceiling by thick chains and a big steel pole anchoring it to the floor. There was also some kind of pulley system tucked discreetly behind a lush stand of ferns in sleek silver vases. She leaned her head back against his chest and tried to take it all in. The mixture of the primitive rock with the ultramodern look shouldn't have worked, but it did.

Her gaze skittered back to the X, and she tensed. "So, umm…is that for me?"

He laughed softly against her head and rubbed at her neck, loosening tight muscles. "There is nothing to be afraid of."

She started to protest she wasn't afraid but decided antagonizing him at the moment might not be the smartest thing she'd ever done. Still, apprehension had her pulling away from him and crossing her arms over her chest. It seemed so stupid, but up until now she hadn't really considered that he might really hurt her. Letting someone she barely knew restrain her sent a jitter of unease through her. True, she didn't see any instruments of torture lying about, but that didn't mean he couldn't torture her with just his hands.

He regarded her in silence, his posture easy, and when she looked into his eyes, all she saw was understanding and strength.

"You know I won't do anything to you that was on your list of nos. You also know I promised to make you orgasm with just one kiss, and I don't lie. I would never do anything that doesn't bring you pleasure. One, because I'm not a sadist, and two because breaking your trust is one of my hard limits."

Her body warmed at his words, and her apprehension faded to a manageable level. Besides, both Laurel and the bodyguard she'd met downstairs knew she was here tonight, and Mrs. Florentine knew as well. She highly doubted her mentor would ever put her in a situation where she'd be sliced up like a lab experiment.

"It's just a little overwhelming is all."

He opened his arms. "Come here."

She did as he asked, sighing when he held her tight and close. The scent and the warmth of him surrounded her. She relaxed inch by inch. Though she felt the press of his erection against her, he didn't try to do anything more than run his thumb over an exposed section of her back in a soothing manner.

"Sometimes I forget that you've never done anything like this. I look into your beautiful dark eyes, and I lose myself." He leaned down and nuzzled her cheek with his, the slight stubble scraping across her skin in a pleasurable manner. "I swear to you, Lucia, that I will bring you pleasure like you've never felt. Sensations that will be beyond anything you've experienced. The only thing I require from you is to enjoy everything I'm offering. Your desire is my desire. Your need is my need. Let me take care of you."

She drew in a deep breath and looked up at him, trying to smile. "When you put it that way, I'm about ready to skip over to that thing and haul myself up."

"Brave, Kitten." His warmth left her back as he stepped away. The tight roll of his ass in his leather pants made her bite her lip as he sauntered over to what she thought was called a St. Andrew's cross. "Come on over. It won't bite."

Now that she'd calmed down, some of her usual spirit returned. She wasn't a blushing virgin, and while she'd never done anything quite like this before, she had enough experience to hold her own. The arrogant, almost amused smile on his kissable lips added fuel to her returning fire.

She lifted her chin and loosened the stays of the robe.

With miniscule muscle movements, she shrugged it off and let it slide off her arms to a silken pool at her feet. His gaze went dark, and the feminine part of her soul purred in pleasure at the predatory shift in his stance. She lifted her foot and kept her toe pointed as she stepped out of the circle of golden cloth with a roll of her hips.

Having grown up in a large Hispanic family that loved Latin dancing, she had a fair bit of experience in how to move her body, and she used that now. Each step was controlled and concise, an elegant flow from ankle to hip. Her breathing increased the closer she got, because it seemed like Isaac was going to pounce on her when she finally reached him. Oh, he may have control over the situation, but she had a feminine power all her own, and she used it to tease him, to dare him to take her, touch her, make her his.

When she reached him, she froze, unsure if she should touch him. They remained less than an inch apart, but he made no move to close the distance. Instead he looked into her eyes, and the bottom of her stomach dropped. The intense hunger in his gaze almost frightened her. She'd never had a man look at her with such overwhelming passion before.

"I'm going to help you onto the St. Andrew's cross. Because this is your fist time, I'm only going to bind your hands and feet to the wood with silk ropes rather than the leather restraints I usually favor."

She tried to seem nonchalant as she nodded, but inside she quivered in both fear and anticipation. Without a doubt he would give her a mind-blowing experience. She just hoped he lived up to his hype. Then again, he'd never actually kissed her yet. God, all that sexual play between them, and they'd never once locked lips. She couldn't wait to taste him, to share his breath, to have him inside of her.

That thought had her stepping onto the cross and

lifting her arms up. It was slightly angled, so she was leaning with her back and butt pressed against the cool surface of the cross instead of straight up and down. She looked up at him, and he reached above her to test a chain. As he did his shirt raised up, and she caught a glimpse of his tight, muscled stomach with a trail of dark hair leading to his groin. Thank God he wasn't one of those guys who removed every bit of hair from their bodies. She liked the softness of chest hair brushing against her nipples, of cuddling with someone who felt like a man.

He reached behind her and pulled out a padded headrest from behind the cross, adjusting it until it fit her so that it cupped the back of her head. She startled when the first thing he tied down was her head to the headrest on the frame with a black cloth over her mask. Dim light shone through the fabric, so she could faintly make out Isaac's form as he moved around her.

Good Lord, this man knew how to set the right mood.

Next he bound her wrists and her ankles. He traced a finger down her calf, and her whole body ached for him.

"Hey, I thought you weren't supposed to touch me except for a kiss."

His dark laugh at once scared and aroused her. Holy crap, she was kinda glad she couldn't see him, because when he laughed like that, he sounded downright sinister. "Kitten, I'm wearing leather gloves. I'm not actually feeling the silk of your skin gliding beneath me, just the slide of leather over a warm, lush surface. You are so incredibly soft. I wonder if you're as soft inside and out. Is your pussy swollen and wet? Your clit hard and begging to be sucked?"

She panted as he traced his way around the body jewelry on her leg. "Yes."

He reached above her knee and stroked the inside of her thigh. Barely touching the skin but driving her crazy. She restlessly moved against her bonds and tugged at them, but they held fast. "You're still too much in your own head, Kitten. I need to help you tune everything out except your body and really listen to what you want. Moan, scream, yell anything you want, and I'll be the only one to hear it, but you won't hear yourself."

His soft leather pants brushed against her body as he walked around her, and she marveled at how much that little touch sent her whole body tingling. It was like she had some kind of energy around her, and it loved his power. Normally she would have giggled at such a weird thought, but damned if she couldn't sense him moving closer to her head. A second later the headphones rested on her ears, and she smiled.

A deep, heavy bass beat came through the headphones, a restless rhythm that would be perfect for having sex. God, the thought of Isaac moving his hips to that sexy beat had her aching to be filled.

Something wet splashed over her belly, and she flinched, then said, "Hey, what is that?"

At least she thought she said it out loud. The headphones were of such a high quality that she couldn't hear anything but the music. It was like being inside a dark club as she watched him as much as she could through the veil. He was an indistinct masculine shape, broad shoulders, flat stomach, and very strong hands.

The answer came in the form of a leather-covered finger spreading the taste of rich red wine in her mouth. She sucked on his finger, licking every drop she could from its surface, wishing it was his big cock instead. All too soon his hand was gone, and she strained to see or feel him.

He rubbed his hands over her belly and spilled the wine lower until it dripped down the insides of her thighs. The liquid felt like a fleeting caress every time he poured, and she tried to see if he was drinking from the bottle as well, flavoring his kiss with wine.

She would love to take the decadent liquid from his mouth, to drink from him like a cup.

The pressure of his hand on her inner thigh had her shifting her hips in an effort to get him to move. To her disappointment he left the apex of her legs and made his way back up to her chest. He wrapped his hands on the delicate metal chains that made the link between her breasts. With one hard jerk, he broke it, and the diamond bra fell from her chest. She hoped he liked what he saw, that her dark nipples weren't too big or too small for his liking. Maybe he was the kind of guy who only liked the unreal gravity-defying actions of implants. What if he thought her boobs were too floppy? What if he—

Her worries splintered into jagged thoughts of pleasure when something clamped down on her nipple and began to vibrate. She knew she groaned, could feel it deep in her throat, but she couldn't hear it. Something about not being able to hear her own passion allowed her to let go a little bit, to let him take more control.

Licking her lips, she then moaned in pleasure as a second vibrating clamp was attached to her other nipple. Then he began to torment her, varying the rhythm, so her body never got used to it. Her hips snapped when he grasped her breasts in both hands and pushed them together. Her empty pussy clenched when his breath heated her throbbing nipples. With a start she realized that she'd closed her eyes and didn't even remember doing it.

His strong hands continued to massage her breasts, tweaking one nipple or the other. Then his touch moved lower, stirring through the wine still on her belly, and tapped unerringly on her swollen clit hidden behind the almost invisible diamond panties. All her breath left her in a gasp, and she cried out as he slowly massaged her through her panties and his leather gloves. Round and round his thumb went until she thought she might die.

If she'd known it would be like this, she would have sought BDSM out years ago. Then again, would she feel like this with anyone but Isaac? No, no one had ever affected her with such intensity, and she reveled in the thought that her reactions were turning him on.

The pressure of his hand disappeared, and she cried out, needing his touch. Wanting his hands on her body, his beautiful blue eyes watching her, his dick deep inside of her and filling her so good.

Cool air hit her overheated cleft, and a moment later something small and buzzing was placed directly on her clit. She screamed and fought the silk scarves tying her down. With a slight jerk, the frame she was strapped to began to move and tilted back until she was lying down. Still the relentless vibrations drove her higher and higher until she wanted to scream.

He removed the clamps from her nipples. She felt so hot, so swollen and hungry for him. The vibrator being held in place by her panties buzzed on. He must have had some kind of remote control, because the buzzing would stop altogether as she neared orgasm, only to slowly build her up again until she thought for sure this time he would let her come.

She pleaded with him, begged him to take her, to do all kinds of wonderfully bad things with her. When that didn't work, she began to yell at him, then beg him, then threaten to cut his dick off if he didn't make her come. Finally she just screamed her frustration. Either her pleas moved him, or he was afraid she was going to pass out, because he simultaneously pressed his lips to hers and held the vibrator down on her clit.

Every inch of her body exploded with pleasure. It felt so fucking good. Wave after wave of bliss tore through her from the top of her head to the tips of her toes until she became electrified with pleasure. She had no idea orgasms could be this good or this long. Instead of ending, her body continued to contract, and her brain flooded her with even more feel-good chemicals.

His mouth caressed hers, and she moaned, opening for him as the vibrator drew more jerking aftershocks from her overstimulated body. This was what she wanted, this connection with him. His taste, his touch, his will had made her feel this way. As she finally began to wind down, the buzzing on her overly sensitive clit hurt. She fought against the discomfort and endured it for the opportunity to finally kiss Isaac. He nibbled over her lips and had her desperately seeking to deepen their kiss.

With a low growl he bit her lower lip hard enough to sting, then gently licked it.

The vibrator turned off completely, and she shuddered when he removed it. More wine spilled onto her belly, and she gasped when the warm, firm length of what had to be his tongue dragged along her stomach, pausing to lick the wine from the indent of her belly button. She yearned to be free, to be able to stroke his dark silken hair, to urge his mouth lower to clean away the wine that surely mixed with her fluids running down the curve of her bottom. When he pulled away, she sighed, partially in contentment and partially with need. Amazing that after such a strong orgasm the act of him drinking wine from her body had tightened her belly and heated her flesh. Usually after she came she was done for the night, but with him, she wanted to keep going, to see what else he could do to her or make her feel.

He untied her legs, then paused to massage her calves and thighs, strong strokes that turned her muscles into mush. Riding an enormous wave of endorphins and delighting in his touch, she barely stirred when he removed the blindfold. However, when the earphones came off, she finally opened her eyes and smiled.

He was above her with his hands braced on either side of her face on the cross. Looking entirely too smug, he smiled at her. "How was my kiss?"

Unable to summon the willpower to smack him, she sighed. "Not bad."

The offended look he gave her sent her into a fit of giggles, and he grumbled, "Let's get you off this thing before you fall and break something."

She grumped at him but allowed him to help her down. Wine ran down her legs, and she glanced down at her feet. "I'm a mess." She giggled again, not sure why she was laughing but feeling too incredible to really even care.

He took her hand and led her to one of the spaces that water rushed down. She almost yelled when he placed her beneath the water, but to her surprise it was warm and felt wonderful. With a laugh she reached up and stood on her tiptoes, letting the water rinse over her. She felt great, amazing even. With one final turn to rinse the last of the wine away, she stepped out of the water and shivered as Isaac wrapped a towel around her.

Without a hint of strain, he lifted her and carried her over to the white fur couch. He sat back and cuddled her in his arms, then tucked her up against his chest. The unmistakable hardness of a very thick erection pressed against her ass, and she froze.

"What's wrong?"

She rubbed her face with the edge of the towel. "I would really like to return the favor. I mean, you haven't…you know. Your stuff is like a rock against my ass."

He laughed, and she hid her face against his chest. "It's called my cock or dick. If you can't even call it by the proper name, you will never get the pleasure of having me slowly push my cock into your soaking-wet cunt. I bet you are nice and tight, all soft curves and heat. Would you scream as loud when you came if I had you on your hands and knees, fucking yourself with a vibrator while sucking my dick?"

While she was embarrassed at his frank talk, her body thought they were all fantastic ideas, and her already wet pussy got wetter. "I don't know." She gave him a seductive smile. "Want to find out?"

He groaned and leaned his head back. "Kitten, you're killing me. A man's control can only go so far, and I'm not fucking you tonight. Now behave, or I'll have a limo take you home instead of me."

She didn't like that thought at all. She wanted to cuddle up into the unbelievably comfortable leather seats of his SUV and know that she could sleep, that he would get her home safe. "I just feel bad you didn't get anything out of it. I want you to be happy too."

"I had a good time as well. How could I not enjoy your abandon, the way you let me pleasure you, and how hard you came? All things Doms crave from their subs." He smiled and caressed her jawbone with his thumb. "But when I said I wanted to take it slow, I meant it. So when you become my submissive, for however long of a time, you will follow my rules. And the number one rule I have with you is to not rush anything, to savor every discovery about your body one at a time, to show you everything BDSM has to offer."

She yawned, using it as an excuse to break the weird tension that grew between them. "Fine. But if I fall asleep here, I want you to make sure no one sees me like this."

He shifted her in his arms and held her close, allowing her to wiggle around until she was comfortable. She couldn't help the contented sigh that escaped her lips as he ran his hands through her wet hair, working out tangles. In a matter of heartbeats, the world faded, and she fell into a satisfied sleep.

Chapter Eight

Brutally cold air blew against Lucia's face, and she awoke with a start. Something tightened around her, and she smelled the world's most delicious cologne. Her mind conjured images of dark silken hair and piercing blue eyes.

Isaac.

She must have said it aloud, because he replied. "Sorry about this. We have to walk a bit to the car."

His arms held her close, and she sighed. "You know, if you carry me around like this too much, I might be tempted to never walk again."

His voice held amusement as he said, "Spoiled, Kitten."

A wave of warmth brushed across her cold cheeks as he slid her into the open door of his car. She took a deep breath to clear her head and pulled Isaac's jacket closer around her. Through the windshield she watched him trudge in the dusting of snow with flurries dotting his dark hair. A blast of freezing air accompanied him as he got into the SUV. Still clad only in his leather pants and tight black T-shirt, he shivered.

Feeling guilty that she was nice and warm in his jacket, she grabbed her hands in his. They felt like ice against her skin. "For Pete's sake, Isaac, you're going to get frostbite."

He tried to tug his hands back. "I'm fine."

Ignoring him, she brought his hands cupped in her own to her mouth and blew her hot breath on them. They remained just as frigid. "Really, you could have pulled the car around."

"And wake you up? No, you're cute and quiet when you sleep."

"That was very nice of you."

He sighed and shook his head. "You almost make me feel bad about what I'm going to do to you."

Before she could question him, he pulled his hands away and thrust them through the opening of the coat, filling his icy palms with her breasts. She let out a breathless shriek and tried to pull away, but her back was against the door. "What the fuck!"

He laughed and traced the undersides of her breasts, then lifted them and ran his thumb close to her nipple, but not close enough. How the hell could she be freezing and aroused at the same time? Was that even possible? It must be, because her never-ending hunger for him sent a flush of blood to her cleft.

Grasping his wrists, she tried to push him away, but he held fast and captured both of her nipples in a hard pinch. "Let me make up for being so cruel, Kitten."

Her protests died the moment he leaned over and opened her coat, fully exposing her chest to his view. She subtly tried to suck in her stomach, and he leaned closer. His hair brushed her lips while he kissed her collarbone. Moving lower, he pressed his lips in the valley between her breasts and let out a low growl.

"Your skin feels so soft, like the surface of a peach," he whispered. "There is nothing on earth to compare with how beautiful you are."

She relaxed a bit, and her pussy continued to grow swollen and sensitive as he lightly brushed his lips over her collarbone and then back down, all the while pinching her nipples hard enough to sting and trapping them between his fingers. He turned his head, and she threaded her fingers through his hair, groaning when he released one nipple from his cruel grip. A sharp spike of pain from her breast made her yelp, but he quickly laved it away with his decadent tongue. Her nipple crinkled further until her breast actually ached to be touched. When he sucked on it, she cried out his name, gripping him closer.

He repeated the same treatment with her other breast, first the pain and then the pleasure. He continued to touch her with restless hands, skimming her waist and hips before returning to her breasts again and again.

"Please, Isaac, please."

He released her nipple with a *pop* and moved back into his seat. "No."

Still swimming in a haze of lust, she tilted her head. "No?"

"No."

Frustration pushed at her desire, and she hooked a leg behind his seat and braced the other one against the console. Feeling more daring and aroused than she'd ever been, she trailed her hand down her stomach and slipped it beneath the tiny panties she still wore. While holding his gaze, she parted her cleft with her fingers and spread her slickness over herself.

She brushed her clit and moaned, arching into her fingers. Isaac watched her with no expression, but the way his lips twitched when she flashed him a peek of her pussy made her empty channel clench with need. What was it about him that made her so uninhibited? She was by no means a virgin, but she'd never been with a man who made her feel this wanted.

Biting her lower lip, she began to rub her throbbing clit in small circles, knowing just how to touch herself to make herself come. She closed her eyes and gasped as her orgasm hovered at the edge. Before she could actually reach her peak, a pair of rough fingers pinched her clit, hard, and effectively ended her orgasm.

She screamed at the harsh treatment and tried to push his hand away.

"I said no orgasm." He removed his fingers, and blood returned to her poor clit in a painful rush.

"As soon as I can move, I'm going to kill you."

He grinned and turned on the car before pulling out of the lot. "I wouldn't advise that while I'm driving."

"Coward," she muttered and jerked the jacket closed before putting on her seatbelt. "Why can't I orgasm? You don't own me. I'll just do it when I get home."

"I'm telling you not to orgasm because I want you hot and needy next time we meet. I want to be able to press you up against the wall and sink my fingers into your tight, beautiful cunt and feel you ripple around my hand." He blew a harsh breath out of his nose. "You have no idea how much I want to pull off the side of the road, get in the backseat, and have you ride me until you can't move."

She clenched her thighs together and cleared her throat. "Here looks like a good place."

He laughed, and some of the tension went out of his shoulders. "How about we talk instead?"

"Fine. Why won't you let me please you in return? I mean, most guys would be begging for a blowjob by now."

"That is a rather personal question. If I answer it, I get to ask you a question as well."

"Go for it."

He tapped his fingers against the steering wheel.

"Because I believe in delayed gratification. Let me put it to you this way. I could have kissed you last night, and it would have been good, really good, but would it have been as powerful as my kiss tonight?"

"Well, no."

"And wasn't your orgasm better because of how long I made you wait for it?"

She squirmed in her seat, the memory heating her from the inside out. "Yeah."

"It's the same for me. When I finally have the pleasure of your hot little mouth wrapped around my dick, it will be all the sweeter because it is something I've made myself wait for, a pleasure that is to be savored and appreciated."

"You make it sound like drinking a fine wine."

He smiled. "In a way it is. If you chug a glass, you're robbing yourself of a better, more intimate taste. Now it's my turn."

"Go for it."

"Have you ever cheated on anyone?" He glanced at her. "Don't lie. I will know."

She stuck her tongue out at him. "I've only cheated once." His jaw tightened, and she sighed. "It was in the third grade. Timmy was my lunchtime boyfriend, and Paul was my playground boyfriend. Then Paul and Timmy met, became best friends, and I lost both my boyfriends."

His undignified snort of laughter startled her. She couldn't help but grin. "No, I've never cheated on anyone, and I probably never will. It's not in my nature." She hesitated but figured if he wanted honesty from her, then she wanted it from him. "Have you ever cheated on anyone?"

"Never."

"How do I know you're telling the truth?"

He smiled, his teeth flashing white in the lights of the

freeway onramp. "Because it's not in my nature."

They drove in silence, and she snuggled back into the seat, her mind racing. She really, really liked this guy even though they'd just met. So far he seemed perfect—too perfect—and she wondered if she would find out he collected Cabbage Patch Kids or had a statue made out of boogers in his bedroom. He turned on a soft jazz station, and she leaned her head on the glass, watching the lights.

She must have dozed off, because all too soon they were pulling up in front of her apartment building. Isaac put the SUV into park and got out. She shook her head as he ran through the cold and opened her door.

Without a word she let him lift her from the seat. Maybe she should give him a gift certificate to a chiropractor for all the time he'd carried her today. All too soon they arrived at her apartment, and she reached into his coat pocket where she'd stashed her keys. With a bit of fumbling and laughter, they made it into her lobby. The rough carpeting quieted their footsteps, and they took the stairs. This time she was behind him and got to watch his fantastic ass work those leather pants as he climbed the steps.

The hallway leading to her apartment was quiet, and she wanted to hold his hand but didn't know if that would be too much like something someone in a relationship would do. Then they reached her door, and she looked up at him, dying to give him a good-night kiss.

Fuck it.

She leaned up on her tippy toes, brushing her lips against his. "Thank you for a wonderful night, Isaac."

He looked down at her and brushed a strand of hair off her face. When she wasn't wearing her heels, he was so much taller than her. He made her feel small, feminine, and desirable. She leaned up and kissed him again, this time a slower brushing of lips that set her blood on a low simmer.

They broke apart, and he stepped back with a rueful grin. "Get inside before you scandalize your neighbors."

"Fine." She unlocked her door and looked up. "When will I see you next?"

"Unfortunately tomorrow I'm booked solid with meetings. I work hard three days a week so I can take the next four off."

"So I won't see you for three days?" She couldn't keep the disappointed tone out of her voice and hoped he didn't notice.

"No. I've decided to take some time off after tomorrow. That's why I'll have to spend so much time tying up loose ends."

"Can you do that?"

He smiled and winked. "I'm the boss. I can do whatever I want."

"Point well made. Good night, Isaac."

"Good night, beautiful Lucia."

Chapter Nine

It turned out that Lucia didn't see Isaac the next day or the day after or the day after that. An unexpected complication happened while he was getting his work caught up in order to take three weeks' vacation. So instead of being able to leap on him the next day, she'd daydreamed about him incessantly. It also didn't help her efforts to get over her crush when he called her every evening on the pretense of talking about the party. While they did discuss the details, they ended up talking more about themselves than anything else. Last night she'd stayed up until past midnight talking about her time in college and what it was like for him to have grown up in such a different world from the one she'd been raised in.

She thought about him while researching what the best whiskey during Prohibition would have been as well as absinthe and champagne fountains. This party needed to be authentic yet fun, so she read books and Web sites about Prohibition until her eyes burned. This morning she'd interviewed skilled carpenters to make a couple of custom pieces she had in mind. One of the carpenters had blue eyes that reminded her of Isaac's.

Her head already ached, and it was only ten a.m. That meant she had at least another eight hours of work ahead of her. While she understood Isaac had his empire to run, she sure as shit didn't envision doing this alone. Her staff was working overtime and then some to get everything ready. She'd told her employees as little as possible about the party, just that it was for a private club, and let them know if any of them blabbed about it, they'd be without a job.

Then she'd given all of them a thousand-dollar cash bonus.

Isaac had suggested that in his nightly phone calls. It made sense; that money would help soothe any irate spouses and reward her employees for remaining loyal to her when things were tight. She and Isaac didn't talk for long, but she still hung up the phone with a huge smile. In a way she felt like she was back in high school with her first major crush. God, what had Isaac been like in high school? He'd for sure have been one of the in crowd, something she'd never been.

The beeping on her phone let her know someone was at the side door the employees used. She checked her security cameras and recognized her assistant, Rita. While Rita was very sweet and could make the most unbelievably lifelike sugar flowers, she had a tendency to be a bit absentminded about the real world going on around her. Things like keys and purses were items she could never seem to remember, but if Lucia asked her to make an intricate sugar-flower bouquet, all she had to do was tell her the instructions once.

"Can I help you?"

Rita squinted up at the camera and gave her the finger. "It is like ten degrees out here, and my ass is about to fall off from frostbite. Let me in, you evil bitch." Her voice came out in a melodic accent that turned her words into an exotic purr.

Laughing, Lucia pressed the button to let Rita into the warehouse now converted into the staging ground for the parties she planned. Her office, formerly the production manager's office, sat almost a story up from the rest of the warehouse, allowing her a great view of what everyone was doing. Being able to look down on her employees working below gave her the ability to keep an eye on everything at once. Rita called it her sniper tower.

The old but sturdy elevator groaned to life, and she made a few notes on the file open on her computer. She'd had to make some executive decisions about things like flowers so she could get them delivered in time. She wanted Isaac to be proud of her and didn't think asking him about every little thing would go far to building his confidence in her.

The squeak of the elevator doors opening made her glance up with a smile. Rita strolled in, and a hint of her delicate perfume flavored the air. She was a beautiful Puerto Rican woman who looked like a goddess but swore like a sailor. However, she was so stunning with her green eyes and light chocolate skin, not to mention tiny waist and long legs, that most men found her foul mouth cute and endearing.

"Thanks for making me stand out there, you heartless asshole."

"Morning, Rita. Did you get my e-mail about the wisteria?"

Rita hung her coat on the rack next to the door and slipped out of her heels and into a pair of house slippers. "Yes. The wisteria will be no problem as long as I can secure a few blossoms from one of our florists. I have the general shape, but I can't get into the *soul* of a flower by looking at pictures."

Lucia nodded along like she agreed, used to Rita's artistic temperament. "Did you find anyone to help you out?"

"Oh, yes. A very delicious young artist from the local university. Enormously talented in sculpting." She sighed. "Such long, skilled fingers."

With a snort Lucia checked her e-mail. "I can't even call you a cougar, because you're only a few years older than him."

"Yes, but women mature faster than men, so I'm the emotional equivalent of a ninety-year-old man."

Lucia's breath caught in her throat, and she clutched her suddenly cramping stomach. There on her computer screen were pictures of her dressed in the next-to-nothing outfit and walking down the stairs of Laurel's store. From the angle of the photo, the cameraman must have been outside the store and zooming in through the big glass windows. Next were a series of images of her being carried into and out of the back entrance of the club. She scrolled down, and bile flooded her throat in a sour rush.

Someone had done a fantastic job of manipulating her face onto a woman in the middle of a circle jerk. It really looked like her, down to the smallest detail. There were a dozen pornographic photos, each more graphic than the next, and they all looked like her.

At the bottom of the pictures was a simple message.

Quit your job as the event planner for the Valentine's Day party, or these images would be mailed to your family, your friends, and everyone that lives by you.

She let out a watery giggle that sounded creepy even to her. "But half my neighbors are too old to own computers."

"Lucia?" Rita crossed the room with a concerned expression. "Are you okay? You look like you've seen a ghost."

"I'm freaking out here, Rita."

"What is it?"

Lucia rolled her chair back and allowed a gaping Rita to scroll through the pictures and note. Rita let out an angry hiss. "Those motherfucking bastards."

"What am I going to do? Should I call the police? I don't want to expose Wicked to the local authorities. I bet that would lose me the job quicker than anything else. Shit, my mom can't see these pictures. She'd die! I mean, fuck, I look at them and think it looks like me! Who did this? Why would they do this? I've never hurt anybody!"

Rita pushed away from the desk. "You call that partner of yours and tell him to fix this shit. Now."

She took a deep breath and tried to control the panic gnawing at her. "Yes, Isaac needs to know."

It took her a few tries to get through her contact list because her hands were trembling so hard. She'd never had to deal with something like this and didn't even know where to start. Blackmail happened to people in the movies, not in real life.

It rang three times before Isaac picked up. "Morning, Lucia. To what do I owe the pleasure of hearing your voice?"

The words stuck in her throat, and she made this weird noise somewhere between a cough and a sob. "Isaac, someone is blackmailing me!"

There was silence on his end before he swore with such profanity that Rita would have been proud. "What do they have on you, and what do they want?"

She took a hitching breath, hating how whenever she cried, she cried hard. No pretty tears here; she got all puffy faced and blotchy. "They have these pictures of me doing some really nasty sexual things. But it isn't me. I mean, it looks exactly like my face, but it isn't me. And they have pictures of me at Laurel's place and then of you carrying me into and out of Wicked."

"Fuck. I will take care of this, I promise." His voice burned with conviction and anger. "I'm sorry you got dragged into this, and I will do everything in my power to protect you and find the people responsible."

Relief filled her, and she took a deep breath. "Thank you."

"I need you to take a closer look at the picture, Lucia. Don't see it as a photo of you, but of someone else, if that helps. Can you identify where the club is if you didn't know? Did they take exterior photos of the club or just the back door? I need to know where they might have been hiding to take these photos."

"Give me a sec and let me look."

Rita handed her a tissue, and she stuck the phone under her armpit as she blew her nose. The last thing she wanted her ill-fated crush to hear was her honking like a wounded goose fighting a cobra. "Sorry, back. Looking at it I can't really see anything outside of us in the spotlight going in and coming out. Everything else is black. They were probably in the woods behind the parking lot."

"Thank you." He took a deep breath. "Now, what are they threatening to do with these pictures?"

New tears rolled down her cheeks, and Rita handed her another wad of tissues. "They said they will send them to my family, friends, and neighbors if I don't quit planning the party at Wicked."

He growled menacingly. The sound made her feel better. There was something reassuring in a primal way about a powerful man being angry on her behalf. It made her feel like she wasn't alone in fighting this. "Hang on one moment, Lucia."

The muffled sounds of men's voices came through the line, and she wiped her face with the never-ending supply of tissues from Rita. He still sounded angry when he came back on the line. "I'm arranging for a helicopter to bring me back ahead of schedule. Don't do anything until I get there, so we can take care of this together. I promise you that I will make this right."

Even though her heart lightened at his words, she

hated disrupting what was probably an important business meeting. "Isaac, you don't have to go to all the trouble of renting a helicopter."

"Actually, I own it. And this isn't any trouble, believe me. If I stayed, all I would be thinking about is you, and I would just get in my lawyers' way."

"Thanks," she whispered and tried to rally her feminist side to protest she didn't need help, but fuck it, she did, and he was the only one who could rescue her like a dark knight in shining armor.

"I'll be there in less than two hours."

"Okay. Thank you, Isaac."

"Two hours, Kitten. Just hold on."

She hung up and blew her nose again before tossing the wad into the basket beneath her desk. Rita held out a mini candy bar from their leftover Halloween stash. She took it with a grateful sigh and let the sugary bliss help her regain her composure.

"Madre de Dios. Lucia, what kind of people are you getting yourself involved with?" Rita pulled over her chair from her desk on the opposite side of the room and sat next to Lucia. "What kind of people am I working with for that matter? Are there going to be pictures of me having sex with a goat or something in my e-mail?"

That mental image helped break the sorrow and fear surrounding her. She rubbed her face and gave Rita wry smile. "I don't know if even that would make your mom bat an eye."

"True." Rita crossed her legs and sighed. "I know you can't tell me much about the club, not unless you want to be taken to jail for breach of contract, but at least tell me it's not a mob place or anything like that. We aren't planning a party for drug dealers, are we?"

She shook her head and allowed the conversation to

distract her from looking at her computer screen. "No, nothing like that. These are all upstanding citizens, the movers and shakers. If you met any of them on the street, you'd whisper and point because you just saw Mr. and Mrs. Famous. The inside of the club is stunning and luxurious, not at all the black-painted basement scene that you see in most movies."

"Hmm, maybe you could get me into this club." She glanced at the screen and raised an eyebrow. "Though I'm not a big fan of a bunch of guys raining spooge on me."

"Ew, what is wrong with you?" Laughing, Lucia minimized the e-mail and felt much better when she didn't have to look at it.

"I'm just saying that all of my dates lately have been booorrinng."

Eager to be distracted from her own troubles, she gave her friend a watery smile. "What about artist boy?"

"He is a space cadet, all big dick and no brains. Wonderful to fuck, but I want more. I want that shiver that you get in the pit of your belly when you lock eyes with the right man. I want that chemistry that makes your pussy wet just to think about them. You know what I mean."

"Oh yeah."

Isaac made her feel like that. She sighed and looked down, regretting her choice of worn jeans and a fuzzy black sweater. She had planned to go visit a local farm to sample their cheese. Now she had to spend the rest of the day trying to figure out how to show those pictures to her family. There was no way in hell she was going to give in to their demands. If popular crime shows she watched had taught her anything, it was that with blackmailers, once is never enough. They will always try to get more.

Her long hair stuck to her cheeks from her tears, and she blew her nose again. After getting a hair band from her drawer, she quickly twisted her hair up into a bun. Her gut churned, but she had to face her fear. "I need to tell the rest of the staff."

"And have all those men you have working for us Googling for pictures of you? You know they're all a bunch of perverts." She snorted. "They'd be running to grab the hand lotion double time. Just wait until your man gets here."

"You are foul, and he is not my man."

"Girl, if he's hopping on a helicopter to come to your rescue, he's your man."

---※---

An hour and forty-three minutes later, Rita buzzed Isaac in while Lucia desperately tried to make herself not look like she'd been crying. If Isaac said anything, she'd blame it on an allergic reaction to peanuts or something. She dabbed a bit of concealer beneath her eyes, then quickly rubbed it in once the elevator groaned to life.

Rita came up and squirted some breath spray in her mouth. "Just be glad you didn't wear mascara today."

The doors to the elevator opened, and Lucia turned and forced a smile on her face. At her first full look at Isaac, her smile became genuine. Dressed in a gray suit and black overcoat that accented his broad shoulders, he looked good enough to eat. Rita must have agreed, because she muttered something complimentary under her breath as Isaac strode across the small space to Lucia.

He cupped her face with his cold hands and leaned down, brushing his lips across hers. "I'm so sorry," he whispered against her mouth. "It's my fault this happened."

She wanted to climb him like a tree, but his cool hands slid over to her neck and helped clear her head. "How do you figure? I mean, maybe it was the old party planner having her vengeance or one of the planners you didn't hire."

Rita piped up from her desk. "Or it could have been

one of your workers that was pissed about you removing the candy machine."

"Hey, they were leaving candy wrappers everywhere, and there were chocolate fingerprints on our table linens."

Isaac looked at Rita and held out his hand while curving his other arm around Lucia's waist. "Forgive me for being rude, Isaac O'Keefe."

Rita came over from her desk with a definite sway in her steps. She looked at him through her lashes, and Lucia swore the other woman simpered. "Charmed."

The only reason she didn't claw the other woman's eyes out was because she knew Rita flirted with anything male but didn't actually mean it. It was just part of who she was.

"Would you mind giving us some privacy?"

The stunned expression on Rita's face almost made Lucia laugh. The sexy woman was used to men falling for her flirting, so to see Isaac not even notice had momentarily hurt her ego. She gathered up her purse and jacket before turning to Lucia. "If I'm getting booted out of here, I'm going to get some coffee. Want me to bring some back?"

Isaac spoke before Lucia could. "No, I'm afraid Lucia is going to be tied up for the rest of the day."

Her cheeks heated, and Rita chuckled, then grew sober. "When you find the motherfucker that tried to hurt our Lucia, you'll make sure they hurt, right?"

"Yes."

"Good."

With that Rita stepped into the cab of the elevator and closed the doors, leaving them alone in her less than stellar office. After being in his penthouse in the sky, he must feel like she worked in conditions that wouldn't be out of place in a Third World country.

"Thank you for coming out here so quick. I hope I

didn't interrupt anything important."

"Nothing is more important than your happiness." He turned away and went over to her computer before she could read his face to see if he really meant it or was just saying the right thing. "Can you pull up the e-mail for me?"

She did, and his expression turned into a cold mask. It seemed like the more emotions he felt on the inside, the less he showed on the outside. By the time he'd finished looking at the pictures and reading the message, his gaze was frigid enough to frost a snowman. "How do you want to handle this? If you would like to resign as party planner, I totally understand and will not hold it against you in any way."

"Hell no." Her temper flared, and she paced around the room. "By giving in I'm going to be doing exactly what they want. Fuck that."

He nodded. "Agreed. I've had more than my fair share of blackmail attempts—comes with the territory—but being that I don't give a shit what other people think, they haven't been very successful."

"So what should I do?"

"Can you free up the rest of your day?"

"Umm, yeah, I should be able to." She blew out a harsh breath. "Sorry, my mind is all over the place. This just makes me so mad!"

"I understand. Let me make a few phone calls. While I'm doing that, do you think you could call your parents and see if they're available for a short visit?"

"What are we going to tell them?" Her heart raced as she imagined her parents' reactions and their disappointment.

He sat down at her desk and looked at the screen with distaste. "The truth. That someone is trying to blackmail you with these pictures, and you aren't going to let them. I'll be there to verify the pictures are false, and the images of you in that delicious bit of gold and sparkle has been edited. Now come here."

She reluctantly went to stand before him and startled when he pulled her down into his arms, the small seat making his hold extra tight. When he hugged her close, she couldn't help the sniffle that broke through. "Is this what it's like to be rich? To always have to watch out for someone following you? Someone looking to destroy your life?"

He kissed the top of her head and stroked her back. "No, it's not always like this, but yes, there are shady people everywhere that don't care who they have to hurt to get what they want."

"Do you have any idea who could have done this?"

"Yes, but I don't have any proof, and I don't want you to go kick anyone's ass without anything solid."

She tensed. "But if you do find out, you'll tell me, right?"

"Kitten, finding out is not an if. It's a when."

They stayed like that for a few more minutes, him soothing her with his gentle touch and her hurt soul drinking up his kindness. She'd never been the type to rely on anyone to fight her battles, but she had to admit it was nice having all of Isaac's resources at her disposal. With a sigh she climbed off his lap. "Okay, let's get this day over with so I can go drink a giant bottle of tequila and make it all go away."

He pulled his cell phone out of his pocket and gave her a wicked smirk that made her nipples peak into hard little nubs. "You won't need the tequila. I promise you that tonight I'll make sure you're focused only on pleasure."

CHAPTER TEN

Isaac drummed his fingers on the steering wheel of the SUV as his private investigator, Edward Humphries, met them outside his office with a large manila envelope. The clouds that had been threatening snow so far just spit out a flake or two, but the forecasters had predicted a big snow later on tonight. Edward was more than a few pounds overweight, but his mind and instincts were the best. Dressed in a thick black goose-down jacket, he hurried over to the SUV, and Isaac rolled down his window.

Edward's thick mustache had a few melting snowflakes captured in it. "Hello, Mr. O'Keefe. I've got the images you requested." His nasally Chicago accent always made Isaac think of football announcers for some reason.

He took the manila envelope from Edward and nodded. "Excellent. Any leads yet?"

"Not yet. I'm going through the mail system right now to see if I can track that e-mail address back to anything we can use." He looked around Isaac to where Lucia sat in the passenger seat. "Don't worry, Ms. Roa, we'll get the asshol—er, I mean, bad guys who did this to you."

Lucia nodded, and Isaac's heart hurt at the pain and embarrassment on her face. "Thank you. Just so you know, that wasn't really me in those pictures."

Edward smiled. "Oh, I know that. You're much

prettier that. Besides, this is obviously a second-rate hack job."

She leaned forward, and her shoulder pressed against Isaac. "Really? I mean, it looked pretty legit to me."

"Here, lemme see that." Edward took the envelope from Isaac and leaned farther into the open window. If Isaac hadn't liked the other man so much, he may have been offended by the way Edward ignored him as he bumped him with an elbow while taking a picture out of the envelope.

Edward started to turn it around but stopped. "Okay, jeez, I feel weird about showing these to a lady."

Lucia said in a dry tone, "Don't worry. I've already seen them, Edward."

"Oh, yeah."

Isaac gently pushed Edward out the window and out of his face. "Just hop in the backseat, Edward."

Lucia chuckled while he rolled up his window. A moment later Edward opened the door and sat in the backseat. They both turned to the private investigator, and Lucia reached for Isaac's hand. It warmed him somewhere deep inside his soul, some place that hadn't seen the light of day in years. He liked that she already trusted him enough to instinctively go to him for comfort.

Edward cleared his throat and dug through the envelope. "So as I was say'n, I want both of you to take a look at this picture and tell me what's unusual."

Isaac was barely able to restrain a growl of anger. He glanced at Lucia out of the corner of his eye. She seemed to be absorbed in studying the image, but her full lips were tight. Finally she sighed and sat back. "I don't see it."

Edward laughed. "Okay, I'll give you a hint. Have you ever seen a group of eight men that all have the same moles, birthmarks, and freckles on their bodies all in the same place?"

Lucia gasped, and Isaac leaned closer. Sure enough, now that he was looking for it, he could see that what was supposed to be a group of men was indeed the same man shown over and over in different positions. He squeezed Lucia's hand. "Let's go talk to your parents."

While they drove to her parents' home, Lucia continued to look through the pictures. "God, I can't believe I'm so blind! I mean, look at this." She held up a photo of her supposedly having sex with a woman wearing a strap-on. "Look at the pixelation around the neck on this one and the shadows. This is totally from a different picture."

He hated to bring up the subject—she'd had enough shocks today to deal with—but he had to tell her. "Lucia, did you wonder where they got the clear pictures of your face?"

She put down the picture and looked at him with her eyebrows drawn together. "What are you talking about?"

His GPS told him to take a turn, and he did before responding. "I think they must have been following you around for at least one day to get pictures of you. Do you recognize your makeup that day? Or maybe how you wore your hair?"

She didn't say anything as she stared at the pictures. The color had drained from her face, and he hated the way her lower lip trembled. "I think this was from yesterday. I wore those earrings, and I had on my bright red lipstick, which I wore before the cake tasting at the bakery. After I ate it was all gone."

Impotent rage made his voice tight. "Edward is the best there is at finding scumbags. I promise when we figure out who did this, they will pay."

She peeked through her fingers at him. "That isn't code for killing them, right?"

While he would have happily ridded the world of people who would do something as shitty as blackmail

Lucia, he didn't want to scare her. Evidently he'd taken too long thinking about his answer, because she groaned. "That was a joke."

He grinned at her. "I know. That's why I didn't answer." She gave him a skeptical look, and he pretended not to see it as he stopped for a red light. "Really, I did."

"You are a horrible liar, but thanks for trying to distract me. So are these people going to be following me everywhere?"

"I don't know. Edward and his team are going to sweep your apartment tonight to make sure there aren't any listening devices or cameras."

She flushed and looked out the window. "Umm, can you ask them to stay out of my bedside table, please?"

He had an idea of what was in her table just by her reaction. He slowed down the car and eased his SUV into a parking space along the curb. They were about a block from her parents' townhouse, and he wanted to hear this. "What's in the table, Kitten?"

"Nothing."

He sighed and turned the car off. "Well, I guess I'll just have to make sure Edward has his team thoroughly explore it." He'd actually do nothing of the sort, but he couldn't help teasing her. A pissed-off Lucia was better than a scared Lucia.

"Don't you dare." She turned to face him, and a dusky blush spread from her neck to her forehead. "It is just some personal items."

His dick began to swell. He leaned forward enough to smell her vanilla-based perfume. "How am I supposed to pleasure you if you won't share what turns you on?"

She looked away, then back at him, her internal struggle clear on her face. Something about his focus on her sharpened, and he recognized that he was rising into his

Master frame of mind. He didn't stop himself this time, because he wanted Lucia to get used to this facet of his personality.

And truth be told, he loved being her Master, even if it was only temporary.

He reached over the seat and deftly slipped his hand beneath her sweater, easily locating her bra.

"What the fuck! Isaac, someone could see us."

She tried to push his hand away, but her lips parted in a soft gasp as he freed one of her nipples. The little nub immediately stiffened against his fingers, and a renewed surge of desire burned through him at her response. He rolled the tip between his fingers, pulling and extending her nipple until she bit back a moan.

"No one can see us except through the windshield, and no one is there right now." He squeezed hard on her nipple, and her hips twitched. "Now, tell me what I want to know, and I'll let you come tonight."

She slowly licked her full lower lip. He thought his cock might explode. "A vibrator."

He smiled and released her nipple only to scrape his thumbnail over it, eliciting a soft hiss from her. "What else?"

"Just that. It's all I need." She shifted her hips and pressed her thighs together.

Unable to resist, he cupped the back of her neck and drew her in for a kiss while continuing to torment her nipple and breast. The harder he pinched, the more frantically she kissed him back. Fuck, he couldn't wait to have his cock between her lips when she was aroused like this.

With deep regret he removed his hand from her bra and slid the cup back into place. Even more reluctantly he broke their kiss and closed his eyes. He rested his forehead against hers, and their unsteady breath mixed. "Stay with me tonight."

She only hesitated for a moment. "Okay."

A strange contentment filled him, and he nuzzled her neck before finally moving away. "Let's get this done with."

As he got out and went around to her side, he tried to analyze why the thought of having her in his bed, of waking up to her softness pressed up against him, made him feel so good. A brisk wind slapped him across his face, but he scarcely noticed it because at that moment he opened the door, and she smiled at him. The pure warmth and sweetness that radiated from her heated him like nothing else.

He helped her from the car and drew her against him. Instead of asking why he wanted to hug her, she wrapped her arms around him and snuggled closer to him. Something inside his chest hurt; then the pain eased. Her scent filled his nose, and he deposited a kiss on top of her head before letting her go.

After brushing a kiss across his lips, Lucia stepped back and straightened her jacket while looking down the street at her parents' house. She groaned and covered her eyes with her hand. "For fuck's sake."

He stepped around her for a better view down the sidewalk and sighed. Waiting about five houses down were a group of Latino men standing at the bottom of an elegant brick townhome. Even from this distance he could see the family resemblance between them and Lucia.

He shut the car door and activated the alarm. "Friends of yours?"

She slipped her hand into his as they started walking. He enjoyed the contact, the feeling of her small hand held in his. He didn't look away as they got closer to the men. He noted that they all appeared to be around his age or younger. They gave him a hard glare as they approached, and he tried to keep from grinning. It was nice to see a family who protected and cared about one another, but if they thought a menacing look was going to scare him off, they were delusional.

"I forgot to mention my aunt, two of my uncles, and about a million cousins all live within four blocks." She groaned as a big red truck pulled up to the curb and another man jumped out, this time a thickly muscled guy with a short red Mohawk. "And that would be Javier, my little brother."

Javier oozed arrogance as he sauntered down the sidewalk toward them. Behind him the other men now split their glares between Isaac and the young man coming their way.

Before Javier reached them, Lucia moved to stand in front of him and fisted her hands on her hips. "If you act like an idiot, Javier, I swear I will kick your ass."

Isaac stepped forward and held out his hand. "Isaac O'Keefe."

Javier looked at his hand, then back at his face. "Hey, fuckwad. Did you knock her up?"

With a shriek Lucia dropped her purse and gave Javier a rather impressive fist to the stomach, hitting the other man just right to knock the wind out of him. As Javier bent over, wheezing and trying to catch his breath, she grabbed him by the ear and jerked his head up. "I am not pregnant! And even if I was, it would be none of your business." She released his ear and stepped back with an embarrassed glance at Isaac. "I'm sorry. Javier…well, he knows better than to say that."

Isaac fought a grin and crossed his arms. "Remind me not to piss you off. Where did you learn to hit like that?"

A flush filled her cheeks, and she turned her attention on the other men gathered out front of what he assumed was her parents' house. Placing her hands on her hips, she yelled, "I'm not pregnant, you gossiping old maids. Go home and annoy someone else." She lowered her head and muttered, "Javier is a Mixed Martial Arts fighter, and he taught me a few things."

Javier gave a weak chuckle. "Worst mistake I ever made."

She held her hand out to Isaac, and he gripped it, noting the slight tremble running through her. Yeah, she was still strung really tight. He'd need to handle the situation carefully to keep her from exploding again.

"Wait," Javier said and stood with a grimace. "Sorry for being an ass, but you're my sister. What is going on? Maybe I can help."

Isaac exchanged a glance with Lucia. "May I tell him?"

She nodded and buried her face in his jacket.

He faced Javier and held the young man's gaze. "Your sister and I have been dating recently, and it has attracted a bit of attention from the kind of filth that will destroy anyone to get what they want."

Her brother glanced at Lucia, then back up at him. "Are you like in the mob or something?"

Lucia giggled but kept her face against his chest. He wound one arm around her and rubbed her back in soothing circles. "No. I assure you all of my business is legitimate, but due to my wealth, I tend to attract the wrong kind of attention."

"No shit. You rolled up in a sick SUV that I've never seen before. Kinda stands out."

"While that may be true, I'm not going to hide the fact I've worked hard and made money."

Javier's lips tightened, then softened into a grin. "I'd be doing the same." The smile fled, and he crossed his arms and tilted his chin up. "Now what's going on?"

"Someone is trying to blackmail your sister with fake

photographs of her in…delicate positions."

Javier's eyes darkened. "What do they want?"

"They want her to quit planning a party we're working on together."

He glanced down at where Lucia pressed her face against him. "Looks like you're doing more than planning."

"What goes on between your sister and me is none of your business."

Lucia turned around in his arms and laid a hand on Javier's shoulder. "Listen, these pictures, they are really nasty. I really don't want to show them to Mom and Pop."

"Let me see one."

She retrieved the envelope from her purse and handed it to Isaac. "You show him."

He waited until her back was turned before pulling out an image. "Well, here is one for example."

Javier swore and covered his eyes. "Oh, fuck. Someone give me some mental bleach."

"Yeah, that's why we aren't sure how to approach this with your parents."

"If you show Mom and Pop that, they will both keel over right there or start throwing holy water at you."

"That's what I figured, but we don't want them receiving these images in the mail and being blindsided." He quickly showed how the image had been doctored. "So you can see that the proof is in the photo."

Javier shook his head. "Put your thumb over her face or something. If anyone else sees this, they are going to flip out and not listen to you. You're lucky I'm the cool one."

Isaac nodded. While it was irritating to have to deal with Lucia's protective male family members, he was glad she had them to watch over her. "Good point. Maybe I can fold the picture so only her face shows or something along those lines. The idea of showing your parents pornography is not on my list of things to do before I die."

Lucia turned around and walked over to her brother before giving him a hug. "Sorry about the sucker punch, but damn, do you really think I would be so careless?"

He laughed and slung an arm around her. "True, plus I haven't seen you bring a guy home in a long time. We were starting to wonder if maybe you liked the ladies."

Isaac struggled to contain a laugh, earning him a glare from Lucia before she turned her attention back to Javier. She went to punch him again, but this time he blocked her with a practiced move and grinned. "Let me go talk with the wolf pack, and I'll see what I can do. In the meantime, why don't you go inside and introduce your man to Mom and Pop. They've been worried sick after your call saying you needed to see them right away. Pop even had Aunt Rosa cover lunch for him at the restaurant so he could come home." He waved his hand toward the group of men standing in a tight cluster and giving Isaac the stink eye. "Hence, everyone in the family now thinking you're knocked up because we couldn't think of anything else that would have put you in a panic."

She glared at her relatives. A few of the younger ones looked away while the older men remained stone faced. "It's like living in a fucking Hispanic soap opera."

Javier laughed. "Tell me about it. Go on. I'm sure someone has called Mom to tell her you're here."

Lucia wrapped her arm through Isaac's and marched up to her parents' house, her chin held high. She started to stop and yell at her other relatives, but he managed to get her up the stairs before she could go off again. Watching her fight with her brother had been like watching a kitten attack a pit bull.

The front door of her parents' townhome was painted a cheerful red, and the steps had been recently cleaned. He tried to ignore the burn of her relatives staring at his back. She knocked on the door, then opened it, pulling him inside after her. The scent of spices and delicious food hit him the moment they came in from the cold, and his stomach tightened, reminding him that he'd missed lunch in his rush to get to her side.

"Hi, Mom, it's me."

A woman's voice came from deeper in the house. "Come in, Lucy. I'm finishing up lunch. Your father is in his den."

Taking a deep breath, she turned to him and fumbled with the buttons of her jacket. "Can I take your coat?"

He brushed her fingers aside and deftly removed her jacket. Taking care of his woman always made him feel good. No, wait, not his woman. Lucia was his temporary sub and business partner. That was it. Still, when she looked into his eyes, he resisted the urge to kiss her to take away her fear. He kept telling himself it was a natural reaction to want to protect the sub in his care, not because he really did care about her.

A lot.

She hung their jackets from brass hooks on the wall of the foyer and led him farther into the home. The walls were painted a warm beige, and colorful artwork added life to the home. The old oak floors lent character to the space. He followed her as she took a left. The way her jeans cupped her round ass gave him very inappropriate thoughts about her right before he was to meet her father.

They entered a decent-sized room with a sliding glass door leading out onto a back patio. Empty pots of various sizes stood grouped together on one end of the porch while a white trestle covered with dead vines blocked the view of the neighbor's yard. Beyond that stood a small yard and a very large plot of dirt he guessed was a garden in the summer months.

A dark-haired man sat on a circular couch facing a massive TV screen. He had a pair of bright blue headphones on, and as Isaac looked closer, he realized Lucia's father was playing a video game. Right now he appeared to be some kind of space ranger taking out aliens.

Lucia sighed and shook her head. "I forgot to tell you my father is a video game addict." She crossed the room and gently lifted one side of the headphones. "Hi, Pop."

The game on the screen paused, and Lucia's father turned with a smile. "Lucy, it is good to see you. Your mother and I were very worried something bad had happened to you. Why didn't you return our calls?"

"Because I told Mom I wanted to talk to you guys face-to-face and that I was on my way over." She turned to Isaac with a forced smile. "Pop, I want you to meet my business partner, Isaac O'Keefe."

Isaac found himself stung at the omission of calling him her boyfriend. God, he was even driving himself crazy with his inability to deal with this situation. Still, he didn't like not being properly introduced. "Nice to meet you, Mr. Roa."

The older man looked him up and down before glancing at Lucia. "From the way my son said you were holding my daughter, I expected you two were dating. I know you wouldn't let a man kiss you in public if you weren't involved."

Lucia flushed and shot Isaac a pleading look, but he just raised his eyebrows. He wanted to see how she would define their relationship, not that they really had one, but it still interested him. "Well, Pop, we've only been on a few dates. It's nothing serious."

Unable to stop himself, Isaac looked down at her and said in a low voice, "It isn't?"

She looked away but not before he saw the longing in her gaze. "I should be asking you that."

Now it was his turn to avoid her gaze. What the fuck was he doing? He had a role to play here, and he was fucking it up big-time. They had more important things to deal with at the moment than his messed-up heart. Life would be so much easier if he just didn't feel anything at all. Then he could continue to be the cold bastard the rest of the world knew. Somehow Lucia had reached past the gates around his heart and touched him.

Lucia's father clucked his tongue. "You kids, always so afraid to be honest with each other." He walked around the couch. "I see it on TV and in the movies all the time. These elaborate mind games people play with each other. Whatever happened to being honest? Whatever happened to—"

A beautiful older woman with silver streaked hair tied back in a bun stepped into the room. "Jose, you're not giving your back-in-my-day speech again, are you?"

Isaac cleared his throat and tried to get his emotions under control. Everything her father said was true. Isaac was playing mind games with Lucia, the same bullshit mind games his ex had played with him. Self-disgust burned through him and helped to clear his mind even if it did make him feel sick.

Lucia's father grumped, but he still kissed his wife on the cheek when she reached his side. "I'm just saying honesty is the best policy."

Renewed guilt singed Isaac, but he managed to keep a calm facade. All those years watching his father run his business with an iron will helped. "I can promise you, Mr. Roa, I've been honest with your daughter about our relationship."

Liar, liar, liar.

Mrs. Roa smiled at him, the dimples in her cheeks deepening just like her daughter's. "Let's get whatever news you had to share with us out of the way so we can go eat. I made *arroz con pollo* for lunch."

He had no idea what that meant, but it smelled wonderful. Taking Lucia's cold hand in his own, he rubbed his thumb over her soft skin. "May we sit down?"

Using as little detail as he could, he let her parents know what was going on. Lucia spoke up every once in a while, but for the most part, she let him do the talking. They sat close to each other, and he found her warmth pleasurable. No, it felt more than pleasurable; it felt right, and that scared him.

Mr. Roa closed his eyes and shook his head. "Why are people so greedy? Why do they want to hurt others to get money? Why don't—"

Mrs. Roa placed her hand on her husband's shoulder. "Lucy, are you okay?"

He turned to look at Lucia and noticed the tears in her eyes. Tears he'd help put there. She nodded. "Yes. Well, not really, but I'm as okay as I can be."

Firming his resolve to keep his emotional distance from Lucia, he pulled her into a hug and tried to tell himself he was playing the role of the man who loved her, not living it.

Lucia and her mother left for the kitchen, leaving him alone with Mr. Roa. As soon as the women were out of sight, Mr. Roa closed the space between them. "Listen, I know who you are, and I know how you go through women. I've seen you with girl after girl at parties, always stringing one along, waiting until they fall in love with you before you leave. I don't want you around my daughter."

Adrenaline flooded his body, but Isaac managed to keep his voice steady. "Your daughter is an adult. Who she chooses to date is her decision."

With a snort Mr. Roa backed up and crossed his arms. "Does Lucy know how many women you've been with?"

He managed not to flinch, barely. "I have not hidden that from her."

"So she knows you've slept with half of Washington, DC."

"What I do with my private life is none of your concern."

"It is my concern because my daughter is falling in love with you."

The words hit him like a physical slap, and he took a step back. "No, you're wrong. It's just casual between us, more of a business arrangement."

Mr. Roa closed his eyes. "*Eres tan estúpido como un perro.*"

"Did you just compare me to a dog?"

"If the shoe fits..." The other man rubbed his temples. "Listen. Lucia is a good and loving girl. Too loving. She trusts people too easily and has gotten her heart broken again and again. But she continues to follow her heart. Not an easy thing to do in a cruel world."

"It's just business," he protested, but the words felt dirty in his mouth.

"For you, maybe. For Lucia, no. She looks at you, and her whole face lights up. My Lucy is not a game player. Keep her out of your circle of friends. She is not strong enough to endure that world." He blew out a deep breath. "Now, let's go have lunch. I won't say anything more—you know how I feel—but if you hurt my daughter, that will be a sin on your soul."

Words failed Isaac as he watched Lucia's father leave the room. A few seconds later female voices raised in greeting. With a heavy heart, Isaac took a slow step forward, the weight of his guilt physically wearing him down. Her father was completely right. He'd been a selfish fool to indulge himself with Lucia. He'd known from the first that she wasn't the kind of woman he normally spent time with. She was soft, warm, kind, and honest while he was hard, cold, selfish, and at times a liar.

His next step brought him closer to the kitchen, and he yearned to go in there, to make it real. He wanted to sit next to Lucia as her man, to be the one who held her heart. Any man would be lucky to be loved by such a beautiful woman. Too bad he didn't deserve her. She needed a man who wasn't all fucked up about love. A man who would love her more than anything on earth. A man who would know he was blessed every waking moment of his life for having her in it.

With his next step he was physically closer to the kitchen, but the warmth it offered seemed farther away than ever. Lucia had a reputation to protect and a family who loved her. He didn't. Oh, his sister loved him, but he lived in DC while she and her family lived outside of New York City, and his parents had passed away years ago. How would Lucia feel if she knew just how many women he'd been with at Wicked? He sure as fuck would be pissed if he had to wonder if every man he passed at the club had been with Lucia. That just proved even more that he needed to get his head on straight and take back control of the situation. The moment he noticed his emotions becoming involved, he should have pulled back and distanced himself, but the lure of her warmth and affection had been too strong. Now she was going to pay the price for his weakness, and he hated himself for what he was about to do.

He reached the curved entry to the kitchen and stopped for a moment, taking in the scene before him. Lucia was setting a steaming dish of food onto a rough-hewn oak table big enough to seat eight. The overhead lights created a soft amber glow in her dark hair. She looked up at him, and he thought his heart might break from the simple joy in her eyes at seeing him.

In that second he knew he would do whatever he needed to protect her, anything to make sure she had the most wonderful life possible.

One that went on without him in it.

It took a great deal of effort to close himself off from her, but he managed. She must have sensed it, because her smile wilted, and she looked away. With his armor back in place, Isaac walked across the room and plastered on a smile that felt like broken glass.

Chapter Eleven

Lucia stared out the window of the SUV as they drove to Isaac's house. After having lunch with her parents, they'd stopped by her place to get some clothes and her laptop. Isaac had been nothing but a gentleman ever since, and she couldn't help but wonder what had changed. It sounded odd even to her, but she wanted the passionate, dominant Isaac back. Her Master. Not the stiff and cold man sitting next to her.

Every attempt she'd made to talk with him had ended up in some boring, inane chatter. For God's sake they'd even talked about the weather. He was driving her insane. Hot and possessive of her one minute, cold and shut off the next. When he'd been holding her in his arms outside of her parents' house, she would have sworn he looked at her with something stronger, deeper than just friendship in his gaze. He did care about her as more than a business partner—she knew it in her heart—but she didn't know why he kept denying it. She couldn't keep up with his mood swings and no longer tried. If he wanted to play the quiet game, she could do it as well as he could.

See how he liked the silent treatment.

They drove through a familiar section of Arlington, and she frowned as they pulled up to the Excalibur Hotel. She should have expected that he wouldn't really want her in his house. He would probably put her up in some extravagant suite where she would happily order two of everything on the room service menu and a magnum of champagne. Well, she'd actually probably cry herself to sleep after indulging in some type of chocolate.

God, why did she always fall for the bad boys? Why couldn't she just once like a nice guy who would like her back and treat her right?

Her curiosity got the better of her, and she broke the tense silence between them. "Am I staying at a hotel?"

"No." They pulled up to a guarded entrance to the parking garage, and the uniformed man inside the booth nodded at Isaac before lifting the gate to let them in.

"Then why are we here?"

"I live here."

She pondered this for a moment, the stupid girly part of her happy that he was taking her home with him while the more mature side of her brain insisted she calm the fuck down. So he was taking her home with him, no big deal. The man lived in a hotel. That had to say something about his commitment issues.

While she'd like to place all the blame on him for her hurt feelings, she had to take ownership of her own stupidity. The man had plainly stated that he would not be getting into an emotional relationship with her, and she had only been fooling herself that there was more to whatever the hell they had between them than business and sex. She needed to take off her rose-colored glasses and really look at the situation. Unfortunately those glasses seemed to be fused to her face, and she couldn't feel anything but anger and sorrow at his abrupt change in mood. Still, she was the one being blackmailed, not him. The least he could do is be civil to her and not freeze her out with his icy silence.

After driving up a series of ramps, they went through yet another set of gates before he finally pulled into a parking spot. From their space on the third-floor parking deck, she could see a nice view of the river reflecting the fading sunlight. After all the stress of the day, she just wanted to sit here and watch the sunset.

Unfortunately, Isaac had other ideas. He got out of the SUV and started to come around to her side, but she opened the door and slid out before he could. He tightened his lips, but she gave him a defiant look, and he said nothing. Irritating him made her feel better, and she brushed past him to the rear of the SUV.

"I'll get your suitcase."

"No, thank you. I can manage fine."

He glanced over his shoulder at her, and her nipples stiffened into hard points. The look he gave her was the one she thought of as Master mode. Something inside of her loosened, and she licked her lips.

He looked away and said in a low voice, "I don't think you can."

She tried to think of a snappy comeback, but nothing came to mind. She wanted him to slam her up against the back of the SUV and kiss her until she couldn't breathe. He said nothing and opened the back, pulling out her heavy suitcase with ease, reminding her of how strong he was. Her body hummed in appreciation when their fingers brushed as he handed her the smaller suitcase. For one moment she thought she detected some humanity in his face; then it was gone.

"Follow me."

She did but stuck out her tongue at his back. Yeah, he'd smoothed everything over with her parents, but that didn't give him the right to be so cold to her. Especially when she hadn't done anything to deserve such treatment. His mood shifts were enough to drive a nun to murder. Normally she would have walked away by this point, but something about him kept pulling her back. It wasn't just the great orgasms, not that they didn't help, but it was more the glimpses she caught of the man beneath the mask. She had a feeling he didn't show that side of himself often, so she believed she'd had a glimpse of some wonderful treasure. Shaking her head at her flighty romantic notions, she watched Isaac walk and wanted to grip his ass with both hands.

Hard. Then bite it until he yelped for making her so crazy.

They walked down the row of cars, and she tried to not be impressed, but there had to be at least ten million dollars' worth of automobiles up here. Cars she'd never seen outside of magazines gleamed and sparkled. She marveled that unlike the rest of the world, the garage lights were actually flattering. Normally her skin took on an ugly yellow tone in parking structure lighting, but in here she actually looked normal.

Well, that must be the difference between the haves and the have-nots. Good lighting.

They reached a set of elevators, and Isaac typed a pass code into the keypad next to the closed stainless-steel doors. When they slid open she wasn't surprised to see marble floors, gilded mirrors, and more good lighting. As the doors slid shut, she took a deep breath, trying to dispel the tension filling her. The only sound in the cab was of their breathing and the occasional rustle of fabric as they shifted.

Staying silent was getting harder and harder, but she was not going to be the one to break it. Next to her Isaac continued to watch the lights on the floor pad light up, but his posture grew more and more tense. What was going on inside his head? Yes, he'd been very clear about not having any romantic feelings involved in what was going on between them, but how could he treat her with such reverence if he didn't feel at least some little thing?

They reached the twenty-ninth floor, and the cab

stopped. Isaac inserted a key card into a slot next to the buttons, and the doors to the elevator opened. She stepped out into a marbled foyer with an elegant circular table in the center. The creamy white marble made up the floor, ceilings, and walls of this space while bright modern art adorned the walls. On the center of the table sat a silver vase filled with exotic orchids of every color imaginable.

Isaac moved past her and looked over his shoulder. "Welcome to my home, Lucia. If you'll follow me, your room is this way."

She startled when she realized this wasn't the entrance to a floor but rather to his house. It wasn't unusual for luxury hotels to have a set of floors that they sold as condos. That must be the case here. How much would something like this cost? Probably more money than she'd see in a lifetime. Isaac headed down a hallway leading to the left, and she followed him past three sets of doors before he finally stopped and opened one.

"I'll give you a little bit to get comfortable." He almost reached out to her, but then fisted his hand and kept it at his side. "There is a room service menu in the top drawer next to the bed. Order anything you want."

"You're not going to eat with me?"

He shook his head and stepped back. "No. I have work to do." With that he turned and went down the hallway, heading in the direction of the foyer.

She stared at his retreating figure before berating herself for sounding so needy. It wasn't like she'd never eaten alone before. Heck, she did it all the time back in her tiny apartment. She didn't even really want him around right now. If he was going to act like this, he could shut himself in his office all night. In fact, she wouldn't eat breakfast with him either.

Wandering into the room, she let out a soft gasp and stared. Floor-to-ceiling windows looked out over the

Washington Monument in the distance. Night had almost totally fallen, but the horizon still held a hint of twilight blue. The room itself was done in soft purple and gray shades, soothing and feminine without being overwhelming. A massive bed with a pearl-gray silk duvet cover sat to her right. In front of the windows was a gigantic white fur beanbag chair big enough to be used as a couch. A purple silk blanket lay folded on the floor next to it.

She tugged her bags in, then absently closed the door behind her, taking in the room from a new angle. A door led off the main room to the left, and she hoped it held a bathroom, because she really needed to use one. Behind the door there was indeed a bathroom. She took care of business before giving it a closer inspection. One glance at the multiheaded space-age-looking shower convinced her that she needed to get clean ASAP.

After shedding her clothes, she stepped into the stall and spent some time examining the keypad before pushing any buttons. There was a command called Mist, and she pressed it to see what would happen. A few seconds later, a mist began to rise from tiny jets located at the bottom of the shower stall. Delighted, she tapped another command for Rain and picked the setting Gentle. Instantly a soft rain fell from the showerheads over her. She laughed, slicking her hair back from her face. For the next half hour she entertained herself in the shower, playing with all the different settings before finally remembering to wash herself. She didn't know where Isaac got his shampoo, but it made her hair feel like silk even while it was wet.

The last drops of water rained down as she turned the shower off before stepping out and grabbing a huge fluffy towel that smelled faintly of lavender. She quickly dried herself and went into the bedroom to get dressed. Using the thick towel, she dried her hair and contemplated her next move. The shower had relaxed her and cleared her mind a bit, allowing her to think about the situation from a less emotional place.

Something about meeting her parents had changed things between them. Her hands froze as she wondered if her father had given Isaac the "be good to my little girl" speech. She groaned and buried her face in the damp towel. Of course he had. He'd been giving that speech to any man she brought to the house since her first date when she was sixteen. No wonder Isaac had been quiet. Any man who got that lecture from her dad wouldn't look at her for the next few days. None of them would ever tell her what it was about, but they'd all had the same reaction of distancing themselves from her.

She fell back onto the bed with a sigh that turned to a moan when she felt how soft and comfortable it was. The mattress conformed to her body, and the silk comforter felt delicious against her bare skin.

So, her father had said or done something to either scare or intimidate Isaac. From that point on he'd been cold to her. She would have thought he no longer wanted her, but for a moment outside of his car in the parking lot he'd been different. She replayed the scene in her mind and tried to isolate what had set him off.

After thinking it over she finally figured it out. He'd basically ordered her to do something, and she'd defied him. Sitting up she smiled and pulled her suitcase up onto the bed, then dug through it and planned her unconventional seduction.

Let him try to ignore her now.

———✦———

Lucia wandered about the apartment in her completely scandalous outfit. Well, maybe scandalous was a bit of an overstatement. She looked down at her breasts jiggling with each step beneath the ultrathin tank top she wore and was glad there weren't any stairs in his apartment. A pair of silky pink shorts rode low on her hips; a good inch of her belly showed. Her long hair hung loose, and every once in a while she felt it brush the small of her back. While this outfit may not be lingerie, she still worked it for all she was worth as she searched for Isaac.

After going back through the massive living room, she noticed a light coming from beneath one of the doors. It took a ridiculous amount of courage to cross the room and knock on the door.

"Come in." Isaac's voice came from the other side.

She opened the door and stepped into a comfortable office. The dark green carpet complimented the cherrywood finish on all of the furnishings and bookshelves. Isaac sat behind a massive desk with his jacket off and his shirt slightly unbuttoned. She could see the soft patch of hair on his chest and wanted to run her fingers through it. Her body grew heavy with desire, and when she sashayed across the room, his gaze turned dark, and he became still.

"I had a question for you."

Giving her a weary look, he pushed back from the desk and folded his hands over his stomach. "What is it?"

She stopped and sat on the edge of his desk, crossing her legs, all too aware of the peep show she was giving him of her bright purple panties. "Why are you acting like such a jerk?"

"Pardon me?"

"You heard me."

His dark brows drew down. "I'm not acting like a jerk."

"You know what? You're right. You're acting like an asshole."

He glared at her and fisted his hands, finally showing her some true emotion. "I would watch what you say to me."

"Why? It's not like we have any real relationship

outside of the club. I'm just here as a platonic houseguest."

The muscles of his neck flexed, but he managed a stiff nod. "Correct."

She swung her leg, making her breasts sway. His gaze locked on them, and her nipples grew to hard points. Evidently they were clearly visible, because Isaac shifted to adjust his dick.

"Well, I've decided I want to try out BDSM for real. I really like it, but I want more, not the pretend Master thing you're giving me. I want a man who is capable and worthy of owning me. Not a fake Dom."

He leaned slightly forward, and the look he gave her almost scared a squeak out of her. "I would once again advise you to watch your words."

With a sigh, she parted her legs and stretched. "Or what? Are you going to bore me to death?"

"Don't push me." He took a deep breath, and his voice came out with a slight growl. "You don't want the results."

But that was just it. She did want the results. She wanted him to exert his will over her, to make her give up control and let him lead her where he wanted. Most of all she wanted him inside of her, moving with her and taking her. And dammit, he was going to give it to her even if she had to provoke him into it to get past whatever her dad had told him to make him back off like this.

"Ooh, big scary man." She looked at the ceiling and tapped her lip. "Do you think you could put in a good word for me with that Texan at the bar the other night? He had nice, big hands."

"Last warning."

Giving him a smirk, she slid off the desk and wiggled her bottom. "I always did want to ride a cowboy."

Even though she knew he was going to move, his quickness still surprised her. One moment she was standing, and the next thing she was over his shoulder and being carried out of the room.

"What the hell?" she yelled and tried to shimmy out of his grasp.

His firm hand smacked her on her bottom hard enough to really sting. "Keep quiet, or I'll be forced to gag you, which will piss me off even more because I want those pretty lips wrapped around my cock, not a ball gag."

Her long hair fell in her face, and she tried to sweep it aside to see where they were going, but she couldn't see much beyond the ground. They left the light wooden floors of the living room and crossed over into the tiles she recognized as belonging in the kitchen, then onto wood floors again. Her bottom throbbed where he had spanked her, but that brief flare of violence had only made her wetter. One of his firm fingers traced up her thigh, and she let out a sharp gasp when he took a nip at the side of her hip.

The world twirled as he lowered her from his shoulder. Before she could orient herself, she was being pushed to her knees. Yanking her hair from her face, she found herself kneeling on some type of weird contraption. It had a kneeler like they had at church, but there was a long section branching off in a T shape. From what she could see, there were all kinds of whips, floggers, and chains hanging from the rich cream-colored walls.

They were in what had to be his personal dungeon. She'd read about them online, but she'd never expected this much...stuff. The space itself was bigger than her kitchen and living room put together, and it was crammed from floor to ceiling with equipment. Instead of the black-and-red creepy dungeon look she had expected, this room was done all in shades of beige, gold, and cream with of course excellent lighting.

Recessed in the wall next to them were glass shelves

displaying all manner of implements. Some she recognized, like the variety of beautiful glass dildos, but others left her gaping in confusion. There was even what appeared to be a gynecological instrument, and she shuddered. No way in hell was that thing going inside her. Below that were a series of drawers that held only God knew what. A rill of fear moved through her, and she swallowed hard, regretting her brainless decision to piss Isaac off.

She was so distracted by her surroundings she'd almost forgotten he was there until he wrapped his fist in her hair and pulled her back, making her arch uncomfortably. "What's your safe word?"

Her mind struggled to make sense of what he was saying. She searched his face, trying to judge his emotions as her trepidation chased away some of her desire. If he was really angry at her, she didn't want to be in this room with him, this place where he could inflict so much pain on her.

She struggled to see his face, her back arching farther, and he loosened his grip and allowed her to look at him. Instead of his usual cold mask, his sharp features blazed with emotion, and her heart softened while her body warmed. There was no anger there, only a lust so savage it made her pussy throb. "Penicillin," she whispered.

"Use it only if you have to. Don't disappoint me."

He released her and fiddled with some knobs attached to the bench. The top part lowered, and he pushed her down so her arms were extended out and her body supported by the bench. She tried to look up to see what he was doing, but the angle was wrong. Something looped around her waist, and she jerked up, only to be pushed back down by a firm hand.

"Kitten, you should have listened to me." He paused and ran his finger along the edge of her tank top; then his touch traveled lower. "I assure you I'm going to enjoy this."

He slammed his hand down hard on her arched

bottom, and she cried out in shock.

"Wait—what—"

Another hard smack had her trying to fight the belt. He smacked her again, but his voice came out even as he said, "Did you really think you could manipulate me into taking you?"

Warmth spread through her in delicious waves, matching the beat of her heart. She flushed and bit back a moan when he rubbed his hand over her butt. Her body ached to be filled, and she rubbed her thighs together, her swollen pussy sensitive to the slightest touch. The scent of leather mixed with his spicy aftershave filled her nose when he leaned down and trailed his lips across her cheeks in a butterfly-soft touch.

"Legs apart." She hesitated, and he whispered into her ear, "Open your legs, or I will stop right now and leave you like this. Needy, wanting. Only I'll secure a vibrator in that pretty cunt that will keep you on the edge of orgasm without giving you relief. Now be a good girl and do as I asked."

Embarrassed but incredibly aroused, she spread her legs as much as she could while still kneeling. His hand slipped between her thighs and cupped her mound, pressing against her clit and making her arch.

"So wet for me." He slipped a finger between her panties and flesh, stroking through her aching folds. "And so hot. You like the spanking bench, don't you?"

She moaned and clenched around him. "*Ay, sí, eso siente tan bonito.*"

He laughed softly and continued to stroke her with maddeningly slow caresses, getting near her hard bud but never quite close enough. "No, you're not nearly hot enough for me yet." He brutally shoved two fingers into her, and she groaned, bucking against his hand. Then his clever fingers found a spot deep within her sheath that felt like he was pressing on her clit from the inside. Pressure built and built within her until she was making incoherent noises of desire.

Right before she reached her peak, he withdrew his hand and spanked her ass, hard. She wailed, the burning of her bottom nothing compared to the need to have him fuck her. That's what she wanted and needed—a good hard pounding to take away all the negativity of the day. She needed Isaac to take care of her, and she trusted him enough to surrender to him.

Despite all of his bullshit, he'd done everything he possibly could to take care of her today. Flying out on his helicopter, hiring a private investigator, and going to her parents' house with her had all been something only a man who truly cared would do. Despite what he said, she knew that he wouldn't hurt her. She could give him everything, even her will, and he wouldn't abuse her trust. All she needed to do was relax and feel, let him guide her, and do everything he asked.

Something inside of her relaxed, and he made a soothing sound as she went limp against the bench, compliant to his touch. The next smack stung, but the pain just added to the buzzing of her body. He murmured softly and stroked her. The faint trail of his fingertips over her body felt wonderful. She gave herself over to the sensation, her world narrowing down to the feel of his fingers. The next thing she knew, the belt around her waist was being undone.

He helped her off the spanking bench, and she almost fell before he pulled her against his chest. On unsteady feet she stumbled back out into the living room now illuminated in moonlight from the two-story windows. Just the act of walking made her moan, and she swore her pussy had never been this tender.

He stopped her before the long white leather couch. Taking her shirt in both his hands, he ripped it off her. Her breath caught at the brutality of the move, and her nipples immediately beaded to rock-hard pencil erasers. She wiggled out of her shorts, standing only in her panties before him.

"Always ask before you take off your clothes. Do you understand me, Kitten? Your body is mine to play with, mine to touch. Even your pleasure is mine to take and give as I see fit." Unable to speak, she nodded and gasped when he palmed her breasts. The heat she saw in his gaze burned her soul. "You are the most sensual thing I've ever seen. So soft, so perfect." He scraped his nails over her skin, drawing a shiver from the pit of her stomach.

"Undress me."

She swallowed hard, and her hand shook as she fumbled with the buttons of his shirt. As his torso was revealed, she grew steadier and moved quicker, wanting to see all of him. She felt like a greedy child unwrapping the biggest box of chocolates she'd ever seen. After pulling his shirt all the way off, she looked up at him. "May I touch you?"

His voice came out in a rough growl. "Yes."

She traced her fingertips over the thick muscles of his chest, admiring his dedication to keeping his body in shape. The flat discs of his nipples attracted her attention, and she lightly ran her fingertips over each, enjoying when they drew tight beneath her touch. He made a strained noise, but she continued to stroke him, to memorize his body.

Moving behind him, she caressed his arms, the firm mass of his shoulders, and his magnificent back. His body was like a study in muscle from one of her biology classes. Pressing her breasts against his back, she reached around his waist and undid the buckle of his belt before opening the button and slowly unzipping his pants.

Instead of going to his front, she knelt behind him and pulled his pants down from behind. As his clothing dropped, she began to lay a gentle trail of kisses down each exposed inch of rugged male flesh. The crisp hair on his legs tickled her lips, but she loved the way his body turned rock hard beneath her touch. It gave her a sense of power to know she was pleasing him, arousing him.

Dragging her tight nipples up his body, she hooked her fingers into his dark briefs and pulled them down, revealing an ass that made her already wet panties soaked. Tight and perfect, the muscles of his buttocks extended up to his lower back. With a soft moan of appreciation, she ran her hands over his hard cheeks, caressing them and watching as he tightened beneath her worship. And it was worship. She'd never been so focused on a man before, and she found his undivided attention incredibly arousing.

Not wanting to lose contact with his warmth even for a moment, she walked around him with her fingertips trailing over his skin. He was so big and solid. She felt very feminine next to him. Looking at him was too overwhelming, so she closed her eyes as she came to his hip. Her breath came out in erratic bursts as she stroked the hair leading from his navel to his groin. Before she got very far, something hard yet rose-petal soft bumped against her hand.

Screwing up her courage, she opened her eyes and gasped. He had a wonderfully thick cock, big enough to please any woman. She swallowed and circled the base of his shaft with her hand, unable to grip it entirely in her fist. She'd never been with a man this endowed before, and she wondered if he knew how to use it. In her experience, having a big dick didn't make a man a good lover. Well, it helped but it didn't make up for lack of skill. Then again he'd proven himself very knowledgeable in how to please a woman, and her need grew.

Stroking him from base to tip, she squeezed out a small bead of precum and smeared it over his thick mushroom head. He grew even harder in her grasp, and she licked her lips, loving how her touch aroused him. There was something powerful about pleasuring him, something that made her stand a little straighter and relax further into the sensual spell he'd woven around them. Even the throbbing of her abused bottom became part of her desire.

He grasped her wrist and pulled her away. "I want you sitting on the couch, naked."

She did as he asked and held her arms out to him, but he shook his head. "Spread your legs wide. I want to see all of you."

A hot flush burned from her chest all the way to her ears. She'd never found her pussy particularly pretty. It wasn't like the pictures she'd seen in men's magazines where all the women seemed to have everything all neat and tucked up inside. Her inner lips protruded past the outer, and her clit was a little more pronounced than the models she'd seen. And she certainly got wetter than anyone she'd ever watched in an adult movie. Even now her honey coated her inner thighs. Would he be disappointed? Did he like really wet pussies?

She must have taken too long, because he grasped her nipples in both hands and pinched them, hard. "I said show me that pretty cunt."

Now that her eyes had adjusted to the darkness the moonlight provided more than enough illumination to see by. Reluctantly she parted her legs a tiny bit and scooted down on the wide sofa. He groaned and she spread her legs a little bit farther, torn between wanting to look at him to judge his reaction and being afraid of seeing his disappointment.

"Wider."

Her thigh muscles trembled as she opened her legs a bit more.

"I said wider."

Anger mixed with her embarrassment. "I am wider. God, why do you want to see me so bad?" Even as the words came out of her mouth, she got a sinking feeling in her gut. "I—uh—I mean, I am, Sir."

His cock bobbed, distracting her and sending a renewed flush of blood to her already throbbing clit. "Do not move."

Before she could question him, he left the room, heading back in the direction of his dungeon. She wanted to look, to see what he was getting, but if it was some type of punishment toy, she really didn't want to do anything else to arouse his anger. Her legs trembled as she imagined all sorts of scenarios, each more unusual and scary than the next. By the time he returned, her breathing had sped until she was almost panting, and her legs did indeed shake.

"Kitten, look at me." She looked at what he held in his hands but couldn't make out more than some kind of long shape and the shine of metal. "Look at my face. Now, deep breath in, slow breath out."

Her lungs expanded on his command, and he talked her through her panic, bringing her back down to earth. "Good girl. You know I'm not going to push any of your hard limits, and you know that I won't hurt you. What are you scared of?"

Embarrassed, she looked away. "I don't know."

He sighed and motioned to her. "I thought we were going to be honest with each other, and you're a horrible liar. Stand up."

The comment about being a liar stung, but there was no way in hell she was telling this sex god about her body issues. She did as he asked, and her nipples tightened to stiff peaks as he walked over to her, his big dick leading the way. He grazed his knuckle down her cheek and cupped her chin with his free hand, forcing her to look at his face. Metal clanged as he tossed whatever he'd brought from the playroom, and with his free hand he slowly caressed the sides of her stomach and ribs, drawing chills from her already overstimulated body.

"You have one more chance to be honest with me before I go back to my study and resume my work."

She'd been ready to fight him, to endure whatever he thought of as punishment, but the idea of him leaving her sent a bolt of pure panic through her system. "I'm not pretty...down there...okay?"

She pushed away from him or at least tried to. He wrapped her in a hug, pulling her to his chest and stroking her back. "Who told you your pussy wasn't pretty?" There was an angry rumble to his voice that made her smile against his chest hair.

"God, I can't believe I'm discussing this with you." She halfheartedly tried to put some space between them, but he tightened his grip.

"Don't you know how beautiful you are?" He gripped her sore bottom, his nails creating little pinpricks of pain. "When you walk into a room, every man turns to look at you and wishes you were his. There isn't one part of you I don't find amazing."

She curled her fingers into the light hair on his chest and nuzzled her cheek against him. It was so much easier to talk in the dark where she didn't have to see him. "Next to you I feel inadequate. I mean, you have the body of an Olympic swimmer."

He chuckled, and the vibrations moved through his hard frame. "I'm actually a pretty crappy swimmer."

Feigning a gasp of shock, she looked up at him. "That's not possible! You're perfect at everything you do."

He gave her a sad smile. "Not everything."

Placing her hands on his shoulders, she leaned up and

gave him a gentle kiss on his soft lips. "I think you're perfect."

Their gazes locked, and the air between them grew heavy with expectation. He cupped her face and brought their mouths together, devouring her lips. Oh yes, this was what she wanted. To not have to worry about how he wanted to kiss her, to let him take the lead. He bit her lower lip hard enough to sting, and she gasped. Taking advantage of her open mouth, his tongue slid in and stroked hers in a seductive dance.

The muscles of his shoulders turned to rock, and he growled. "You taste so good. Let me taste all of you, Kitten."

Her body vibrated with need. The thought of his talented tongue between her legs made her knees weak. "Okay."

He swatted her behind, and she yelped. "Hey!"

"Is that how you answer me?"

Licking her lower lip she looked at him through the veil of her lashes. "Please, Master, would you give your humble slave the pleasure of your tongue."

His gaze flared, and she took in a deep breath. "Stay standing."

Confused, she watched him pick up the bar with two strappy-looking things hanging off it.

"What is that?" He glanced at her with raised eyebrows, and she flushed. "I mean, what is that, Master."

"Say it again."

"What—"

"No, call me Master."

The word took on new weight and meaning in her mind. She forced herself to meet his eyes. "Master."

"Who do you belong to, Kitten?"

The logical part of her mind yelled she didn't belong to

anyone, especially to a man who would dump her in two weeks' time. But the hedonistic side of her nature shut the door on logic and opened her soul to the enigmatic man watching her so closely.

"You, Master."

Without another word, he knelt before her and began to strap one of the restraints around her upper thigh. When it was cinched tight, he moved to her other leg and tapped it. "Widen your stance."

Using his shoulder to balance herself, she did as he asked. The cool air brushed over the wetness of her cleft, and she tried to close her legs, but he bit her inner thigh hard enough to sting. "Keep your legs open, or I'll tie you up, stick vibrators all over you, and make you orgasm until you can't take it anymore."

She gasped as heat flared in the pit of her stomach.

He chuckled and secured the other strap on her upper thigh, right below her bottom. "Well, I see that idea intrigues you."

She tried to move her legs, but the short bar that spanned the distance between the backs of her legs kept them open. "What is this thing?"

"It's a spreader bar. There are all different kinds, but this one keeps you open to me without hindering my access." He swirled one finger through her wet folds, and she groaned, glad she had his shoulder to brace herself on. "Now, we know you enjoy vibrators, but what about anal toys?"

The tip of his finger brushed over her clitoris, and she keened softly. "I've never done that kind of stuff, Master." The more she said it, the easier it became. Master. Her Master.

"No one has ever taken you anally?"

She shook her head and tried to tilt her hips to make

him stroke across her throbbing button again. "No, Master." Her mind piped up that good girls didn't let men play back there, but the emerging submissive side clapped with glee at the thought of her Master touching that forbidden area.

"But you will allow me to do as I see fit? To put anal beads into that sweet, round ass?" He pushed his finger into her entrance and groaned. "You are so hot and wet."

"I— Oh God, I'll do anything you ask, just please make me come."

His breath blew gently on the neatly trimmed curls over her mound. "I like how you keep the lips of your pussy bare. It gives me such a soft, smooth surface to touch."

"I'm glad you like it, Master." Right now she'd shave her pubic hair into any shape he wanted if he would touch her more. "Please...I need you."

"How much?" He nuzzled his cheek on her inner thigh, and she delighted in the scrape of his stubble.

"More than I've ever wanted anyone, ever."

He kissed her inner thigh. "You are sweet."

She protested when he stood, but he merely smiled and lifted her into his arms before depositing her on the couch. The spreader bar made it impossible to walk or close her legs, but that didn't stop her from trying. Being completely open to his gaze made her feel both aroused and uncomfortable. Her mind shifted between the two feelings like a coin spinning on a table.

He shook his head and knelt before her. "You have a beautiful pussy, and your clit is nice and hard for me, peeking past its soft hood and begging for my mouth." He placed a chaste kiss on her hip, then looked up at her, capturing her with the honesty in his gaze. "Lovely."

His words loosened the knot of anxiety and allowed her desire to come roaring back to life. Moments before she'd felt awkward about being in this position, but how could she be embarrassed when her body obviously aroused him? He continued to hold her gaze, and the air became charged between them, filled with unspoken pleas on her part and promises on his.

"I can't wait to taste you, but first, play with your nipples for me. I want to see you touch those pretty tits."

A groan rose from deep in her body, and she relaxed back into the cushions. Normally she wasn't one for dirty talk, but when Isaac did it, the words inflamed her, made her wanton. She pinched her nipples between her fingers and pulled on them, crying out as the sensation blended into the empty ache of her body.

"Good girl. Now do it harder. Pretend it's my hands on you, my fingers tormenting you."

"Oh fuck," she gasped and did as he asked. Each tug and pinch seemed to connect to her groin until it almost felt like she was touching her clit each time she rolled her stiff peaks between her fingers. The sensations soon became too much, and she rocked her hips as best she could. "Please...Isaac."

"Easy, Kitten. I intend to savor you, and no matter how prettily you might beg, you aren't going to force me to do anything. I'm in charge of your pleasure. I make all the decisions. The only thing that I ask of you is to sit back and feel. Shut that busy mind of yours down and focus on your body."

He trailed his fingers along the edge of her hip, barely caressing her. A sizzling path of tingles followed in the wake of his stroke, setting fire to her skin. She closed her eyes, unable to take the intensity of his gaze. He made her feel so vulnerable, so needy. The pleasure from his touch surely had to be addictive.

"Look at me."

The command in his tone made her weak. Licking her

suddenly dry lips, she opened her eyes. He grinned at her, and she whimpered. There was such decadent sensuality in his eyes. Everything about him was a visual feast, from his perfect features to the light trail of dark hair leading down from his chest to his cock. The thought of him being inside of her, taking her, had her squirming.

Instead of lowering his head between her thighs like she expected, he reached beneath her and grasped the bar resting against the lower curve of her buttocks. Before she could ask him what he was doing, he jerked her up and forward. "Put your legs over my shoulders."

A tremor shook her, and she was pretty sure if she became anymore aroused, she'd have a stroke. With his help, she put one leg over each of his shoulders. He maintained his grip on the bar beneath her and tugged her toward him so that her bottom completely left the couch, and her weight was balanced on her upper back and shoulders.

Holding her gaze he lifted her lower half using the spreader bar and brought her aching sex up to his mouth. Then he ever so slowly licked her from the entrance to her sheath all the way to her clit.

"You taste like the sweetest sin."

She gripped the couch as he did it again. "Oh God, oh fuck."

He smiled and nipped at her aching bud. "Eyes on me, Kitten. I want you watching me enjoy myself." He took another lick. "Delicious."

Tracing his tongue along the seam of her sex, he growled. That sound vibrated against her flesh. Her heels dug into his firm back, but she couldn't close her thighs. She couldn't stop him from what he was doing and had no choice but to enjoy the sensations his über-talented mouth was creating between her legs.

So fucking hot.

His fingers flexed beneath her bottom, and he slowly rocked her back and forth on his tongue, lowering and lifting her with the bar. She fell into his rhythm, and her breathing grew short and uneven. Back and forth, up and down, he tormented her flesh with an expert touch. Suddenly he held her still and blew on her swollen sex, eliciting a groan.

"Do you want to come, Kitten?"

She tried to force her mind to think and her mouth to work, but neither was responding. Instead she nodded and groaned.

He chuckled and let go of the bar, instead supporting her weight by cupping her bottom. "I love a woman with curves, with softness to grab and hold on to."

He squeezed hard, and she bit her lower lip. Without preamble he lowered his head and began to suckle on her clit. A roaring wave of heat screamed through her body. Every single muscle from her head to her toes tensed. He rubbed his tongue up one side, then down the other of her pulsing bud, then sucked again. The way he tormented her, it was like he knew her body better than she did.

"*Dios mío, eres tan bueno.*"

Words spilled from her in a torrent of incoherent whispers. Her mind had gone on vacation, leaving behind her ravenous libido to run things. She'd do anything he asked, anything as long as he would give her an orgasm.

His teeth grazed her hood, and she groaned in frustration. "Do you know how sexy it is to hear you speak in Spanish when you're aroused? Music to my ears." He flicked her clit, and she jumped in response. "And the Dom in me loves it when you surrender to me. I can do anything I want to you because you trust me. You've pleased me very much."

Unable to face the intensity of his gaze, she closed her

eyes and stroked her breasts, knowing he liked that. Being aware that she was bringing him pleasure was almost as great of an aphrodisiac as receiving, and she quickly approached her orgasm at the first brush of his lips.

"You can come for me now, Kitten. And I want you to scream while you do it."

Before she could take a breath, he penetrated her with two fingers and sucked on her clit. She exploded around him, her orgasm turning the world a brilliant white behind her eyelids. It flowed through her like a flash flood, sweeping away every thought and filling her with joy until she thought she might burst. He continued to lightly suckle her flesh. She twitched and moaned beneath his onslaught, whispering his name over and over again.

Isaac, her Isaac.

Chapter Twelve

The taste of Lucia—red wine with a hint of salt—filled his mouth. Delicious. He could feast on her all day, but his little Kitten was looking a bit shell-shocked. She stared up at him with wide, dark eyes while her magnificent breasts trembled with each breath. The vulnerability in her expression stirred feelings in him he thought he'd gotten rid of. He pulled back from her swollen and hot pussy, aching inside to burry himself in her. But he couldn't. No, sex with Lucia would lead to complications he couldn't afford right now.

She was off-limits.

He unbuckled her thighs and placed a kiss on each, rubbing his face against the warmth of her skin. She was so smooth, so lush. Touching her was like running his hand over an expensive bolt of the finest silk. Her leg shook as he nipped her tender skin, and he smiled, loving how responsive she was. Her reactions weren't contrived or forced. He'd forgotten how nice it was to have a woman who was new to the lifestyle.

Removing the spreader bar from behind her legs, he massaged her tense muscles, and her whole body melted into the couch. If he wasn't mistaken, his Kitten was purring with pleasure. With great reluctance he removed her legs from his shoulders. She stirred and gave him a blissful grin.

"Wow." The breathless and husky sound of her voice made his balls draw up tight. "Thank you."

She wrapped her arms around him and nuzzled her face against his chest. He was used to being the one who initiated all the moves, so her honest response knocked him off balance. She was so soft and warm; there was no way he couldn't return her open affection. She began to place soft kisses all over his chest, then paused to lick at his nipple. "You made me feel so good. Now let me make you feel good, Master."

Irritated by the emotions flooding his body, he stood up and pulled her off the couch until she was on her knees before him. There, now things were back like they were supposed to be. He intended to be rough and crude to break the forbidden connection between them, but instead he said, "You have no idea how much you please me, Kitten."

A wicked gleam entered her eye, and she licked her lips. "Your Kitten wants some cream."

Her saucy comment startled a laugh out of him, but he placed a hand on her shoulder to keep her from bringing those full, fuckable lips near his cock. "I want you to swallow every drop, to suck me dry. I'm going to fuck your face, Kitten, and come down that smooth throat of yours."

She gasped, and her hips tilted forward. Well, it looked like Ms. Lucia needed another orgasm. He loved a woman with the stamina to keep up with him. He wrapped his fist into her silken hair and held his cock steady with the other. Carefully, he guided her head to his erection and groaned when she licked at the tip. This was torture, absolute torture.

With a happy sound, Lucia opened wide and began to inch him into the hot, wet confines of her mouth. He loved the feeling of how her small hands encircled his dick as she suckled on the head, doing a little swirling motion with her tongue that drove him wild. Then she squeezed the base of his shaft hard and fit as much of him into her mouth as she could, gagging slightly. God dammit, her throat convulsing against the sensitive head of his cock almost made him shoot right there and then.

Using her hair, he pulled her back and tried to cool down. Coming in her mouth thirty seconds after she touched him so wasn't going to happen. "Lick my balls."

The soft stroke of her small tongue against his sac made him shudder. She licked him as if cleaning him, leaving no part of his sensitive flesh untouched. He tugged on her hair, and she licked her way up to his shaft, moaning deep in her throat as she traced the veins with the tips of her fingers. Her light, teasing touch almost undid him, but he wasn't finished with her yet.

He wanted to fuck her so badly, but he just couldn't. It wouldn't be fair to her. That would only encourage her to think that there might be something more than just sex between them, because he sure as fuck couldn't be inside of her and hide his fucked-up feelings. It wouldn't be right to be buried balls-deep in her hot pussy, to feel her clench him as she came again and again. She was addictive, and right now he was skating on the edge of becoming a full-blown junkie. Dragging her up by her hair, he forced her to stand and tilted her head before kissing her. Her full lips parted for him, and he nibbled on her lower lip while she cried out and rubbed her hips against his erection.

Not breaking their kiss, he led them back to the couch, and he released her hair. She stared up in him with wonder shining in her dark eyes. Dammit, when she looked at him like that, it made him feel ten feet tall, like he could and would conquer the world to keep the woman in his arms safe and happy. He sat on the couch and patted his knee.

"Come here and straddle me."

She hesitated and twisted her fingers together. "Do

you have protection?"

"I'm not going to fuck you, Kitten." Every time he said that, it sounded less like he meant it. "Besides, I'm tested regularly and always use protection." He licked his lower lip, and her eyes followed the movement of his tongue. The taste of her was still fresh in his mouth and sent a carnal bolt of lust to his loins. "And I know from the medical records that you submitted as part of your forms for Wicked that you are clean and on birth control."

She moved a step closer and stood in between his legs. He closed his thighs and trapped her there. "While my mind seems to disappear when I'm around you, I would never do anything to endanger you." He opened his thighs. "Now straddle me."

The silken glide of her skin over his legs was both heaven and hell. He was determined to get her off one more time before he came. Later they'd work on seeing how many orgasms she could have in one night.

The shift of her hips broke his thoughts, and his cock rested between his stomach and her pelvis. He grasped her waist and pulled her closer until their lips were almost touching. Her soft pants warmed his mouth, and her pussy was soaking his lap. She was so very, very wet. He loved it.

"Now, I want you to stroke yourself up and down my dick. Rub that sweet little pussy all over me, but do not sheathe me."

Her whole body shivered, and he smiled against her mouth. So responsive. Then she began to move, and he nearly lost his mind. Hot, slippery, divine, she rode him with long strokes that caressed his aching prick from base to tip. When she reached the top, he held her still and slowly rubbed the tip of his erection over her hard clit, drawing mewling cries from her.

She wrapped her arms around him and placed small kisses all over his neck and shoulders, her scent filling the air around him with the most delicate of perfumes. They moved together, and she tried to pick up the pace, but he held her steady, drawing it out, making her work for it. Her movements grew erratic, and she sought his mouth.

"*Acabame, ya no aguanto.*"

He groaned and cupped one hand around the back of her neck and her full ass with his other. Their tongues met and slid against each other as he pressed her closer to his cock. He wanted to come so fucking badly, to paint her beautiful caramel skin with his seed, but her needs came first.

Not breaking their kiss, he began to inch his fingers over to the seam of her butt. She groaned and wiggled, sorely testing his self-control. God, he wanted his cock inside her tight ass as well, to be inside of her and make her his. To be the only man who got to taste and enjoy this amazingly beautiful woman. Reality tried to intrude in the form of his mind yelling at him to keep his distance, but he told it to shut the fuck up.

She tensed, and he ever so gently pushed the tip of his finger into her tight hole. She tried to pull away from their kiss, but he wouldn't let her, claiming her mouth and jerking his hips so she was trapped by him, forced to endure the pleasure. When he pressed deeper into her ass, she whipped her head back and screamed his name, her sweet pussy quivering against him as her muscles contracted and released again and again. He groaned as her cunt gushed a fresh wave of honey over his dick.

She collapsed against him. "I had no idea it could be so good."

He rubbed his aching shaft against her softness. "Suck me off, Kitten."

With a wicked if slightly dazed smile, she slid down his lap and took him as far as she could down her throat with one swallow. The sensation bowed his back, and she fondled his balls, stroking them as she sucked. There wasn't a man on earth who could last long against her oral skills, and he didn't even try.

The burn of his release threatened. One more clever flick of her tongue, and she was struggling to swallow his load, licking and sucking at the mushroom head of his cock as he spurted jet after jet into her eager mouth. Her little humming sounds of pleasure drew another surge from him. She continued to gently lick him, easing him down from his orgasm and keeping him in a state of semierection. She gave a final delicate swipe with her tongue on the sensitive underside of his dick, and he moaned.

She sat back on her heels, beauty personified, and smiled shyly. "Did I do okay?"

The uncertainty in her gaze pulled at his heart, and he couldn't stop himself from standing and helping her to her feet. "Sleep with me tonight."

A slight frown marred her lips, and a little line appeared between her eyebrows. "I thought you said no fucking."

The word sounded crude on her tongue. He didn't like it, and that just showed how far he was in over his head with her. When a man thought only of making love to a woman instead of fucking her, shit was serious. Still, he could no more resist the need to have her pressed against him, to hold her and lose himself in her scent than he could resist his next breath.

"Just sleep, no sex." He pulled her into his arms, and she sighed against him, her tense muscles going loose. "Only a fool would sleep alone when there is such a pretty kitten to cuddle."

She giggled and bent to retrieve her clothing, giving him an eyeful that made his cock twitch. He held out his hand; she slipped her fingers into his, a small smile curving her lips and making her look mysterious. As he led her through the apartment to his bedroom, it occurred to him that he'd never had a woman in his bedroom. In fact, he couldn't remember the last time he'd had a woman in any part of his house except his dungeon.

They reached his room, and he opened the door, bemused at how she tried to use her scant clothing to cover her breasts and pussy. Then she caught a glimpse of his room and gasped. He followed her in, watching her examine the cream watered silk wallpaper and trace her fingers over the pattern. A dim light glowed from his nightstand and highlighted the curve of her waist. Her skin glowed as if she'd been dusted in gold.

She made her way around the room, stopping to look at pictures of his family on the mantel above his fireplace before looking at his bed out of the corner of her eye.

"Umm, may I use your restroom?" Her voice came out in a nervous squeak.

He grinned and enjoyed her blush. "It's that door right to your left."

She nodded and scurried into the bathroom. While she was taking care of business, he pulled down the covers of his bed, and he felt…happy. In fact, he felt more than happy. He felt almost light-headed, blissful. It was as if his post-orgasm glow had grown stronger instead of receding. He frowned down at the mound of pillows at the head of his bed. Did she feel this good? Had he made her body ring like a bell?

Christ, he was acting like a besotted schoolboy. Shaking his head, he slid between the smooth sheets and tossed a few pillows to the side in order to make room for Lucia. Whenever a woman had asked to spend the night before, he'd brushed her off, not comfortable with the idea of her being in his personal space. Now look at him, fluffing pillows for a curvy little slip of a girl.

The door to the bathroom opened, and she held a towel

to herself. "Do you have a T-shirt I could borrow to sleep in?"

The idea of her wearing something of his pleased him. "Sure, the closet is behind the door to your left there. Look in the dresser immediately to your right. First three drawers."

She arched her brows. "You have three drawers of T-shirts?"

"I buy T-shirts from everywhere I've been." Her lips twitched, and now it was his turn to raise his brows. "What?"

"Oh, nothing. I guess I never pictured you doing something so normal. I thought maybe you collected Fabergé eggs or golden statues."

She darted into the closet before he could reply. If she were his sub, she'd find herself spending a great deal of time spread over his lap getting spanked for her sassy mouth. The idea stirred his libido, and he shuffled around the blanket to hide his erection. God, he couldn't be around her without wanting her. Having her sleep with him was a bad idea. He should claim some kind of work emergency and go downstairs.

Yep. He was going to leave. Any second now.

When she came out of the closet, he still hadn't moved an inch, and as he gazed at her in his oversize purple T-shirt from Monaco, his heart lurched. Disheveled, uncertain, and shy, she clasped her hands together and looked up at him from beneath her lashes. "Is this one okay?"

"Kitten, you look like every man's wet dream."

She smiled and to his shock took a running leap onto the bed, bouncing among the pillows with a wonderful giggle. "Oh my God, this bed is amazing."

He watched in amusement as she rolled back and forth, wiggling around until she'd scooted beneath the covers and curled up next to him. A stray curl of her dark hair obscured part of her face, and he brushed it back, enjoying how her eyes half closed at his touch.

"Feel better?"

"Mmm. If I felt any better, I might float away."

He threw his leg over hers and pulled her closer. "I'll have to make sure to keep you tethered to me." The image of her kneeling before him, accepting his collar, ran through his mind, but he tried to ignore it.

He clapped twice, and the lamp next to him turned off. She stiffened against him and began to make odd noises. Her body shook, and he clapped twice again, turning the lights back on. When she looked up at him, he was afraid he'd see tears, but instead they shone with suppressed laughter.

"What?"

She whispered, "You have a Clapper?"

He stiffened and tried to give her his best imposing Dom look. "I don't like having to roll across my bed to turn out the lights."

She nodded, then turned and buried her head in the pillows and laughed.

"What? It's a very practical invention."

Her howls of muffled laughter amused and annoyed him, so he pinched her wonderfully round ass. "I would suggest you not laugh at the man with the paddle."

She peeked one eye at him and snorted. "Tell me, when you spank someone in here, does it look like a strobe light?"

He stared at her, then began to laugh. "I see your point, but no, I've never had a submissive in here."

Her eyes grew wide, and the laughter faded from her face. "Really?"

Uncomfortable, he clapped the lights off again and ignored her snickers. "I've never seen the need."

She cuddled close again, wrapping herself around his stiff frame like the world's most comfortable blanket. They lay together in silence for a little while, and she stroked his chest while he rubbed his fingertips along the exposed portion of her lower back where the shirt had ridden up. This felt amazingly good. He never knew it would be so satisfying to have a woman in his bed, to know that her scent would be trapped beneath the covers, that she trusted him enough to sleep with him.

Her voice, low and husky, came through the darkness. "Thank you."

"For what?"

"Everything." She stiffened but continued to touch his body. "I mean, I know this isn't permanent or anything, but man, you know how to show a girl a good time."

He smiled even as his gut tightened at the thought of never seeing her again. "I aim to please, Ms. Roa."

"Mmm. Me too."

Her breathing evened out, and her touch slowed, then stopped. To his amusement, she softly snored before changing position, turning in her sleep and pulling his arm with her until he was on his side, curved around her and sinking into her comfort.

His dreams were disturbed by the sensation of softness pressed up against him or more specifically up against his now hard dick. Still half asleep, he reached out and grabbed the shape next to him, delighting in the feel of feminine curves. Even better, she smelled divine. He burrowed his nose into the hair at the base of her neck and inhaled deeply.

Lucia.

His mind whispered the word, and images of a voluptuous Hispanic woman danced through his head, hardening him further. So beautiful, so sweet. She wiggled back against him, and he growled, setting his teeth on the side of her neck. With her back pressed to his front, her ass grinding into his cock, she fit perfectly in his arms. Her gasp and murmur of pleasure inflamed his blood.

Reaching down, he coaxed her legs apart, lifting her thigh over his hip. Her tiny panties were easy enough to push aside, and he was gratified to find her cunt wet and ready for him. She bucked when he circled her clit with his thumb and rubbed that delicious ass against his bare cock. Dimly he wondered why Lucia was in his bed, but the why didn't really matter. She was here, and she was his.

Slowly he tormented her, pushing one, then two of his fingers into her wet heat. Her breathing became erratic as he slowly finger fucked her, continuing to nibble against her neck.

"Please, Isaac—Master, please," she cried out when he withdrew his hand.

"Beg for it."

"Oh please. I need you so much."

Such a sweet little sub. Maybe this once he could have her. Yeah, that would get her out of his system. It was the anticipation that made her seem so incredible. Plus, if he didn't sink his cock into her and take her, he'd lose his mind.

In a swift move, he rolled her over to her stomach and spread her legs. In the slivers of sunlight streaming into his bedroom from the curtain-covered windows, she looked flawless. He hadn't been lying when he said her cunt was pretty. Swollen and puffy, dusky on the outside and oh so pink on the inside. He swirled the tip of one finger between her folds, parting her lips and drinking in the sight of how wet she was. She arched for him, exposing herself further.

Fisting his cock, squeezing it hard to keep from coming, he rubbed the head against her entrance.

"Is this what you want, Kitten?"

"Yes, please."

He hesitated. "Do you want me to use a condom?"

"No, protected and clean like you. God, please, Isaac!"

She made an inarticulate noise against the pillows, his T-shirt pushed up her back and her hair a disheveled mess. Closing his eyes, he allowed himself to slowly push the head of his cock into her. Like a tight fist she clenched around him and groaned. She tried to push back, to take him all the way, but his hand around his erection stopped her.

"Tell me what you want."

She threw her hair over her shoulder and looked back at him, her eyes blazing with passion. "I want you to fuck me. I want that magnificent cock inside of me."

"Such a good girl."

He hauled her hips up higher and grabbed a couple pillows, putting them beneath her so that she was as wide open as she could be. Unable to resist, he leaned down and licked her sex like an ice-cream cone, bringing forth a new rush of her honey. He used the stubble on his chin to scrape over her clit, and she shuddered.

Gripping her hips, he angled himself and began to sink into her, fighting her tight body to let him in. She went still beneath him, her breath coming out in rapid pants. He kept up his slow slide, and sweat broke out over his body as he tried to restrain the urge to slam into her. She wasn't ready for that, yet.

Finally he was seated all the way, his balls hitting her clit due to the angle he had her at. Her pussy throbbed around his dick, seeking to milk him dry. One slow slide out, then back in, repeating the motion and pace until she once again began to writhe beneath him. God, she was sexy when she was being fucked. She'd turned her head to the side, and her eyes were closed, her full lips parted and soft. The memory of her eagerly swallowing his load yesterday did nothing to cool him down, and he picked up the pace.

He shoved his hand between the pillow and her pussy, rubbing her clit until she tensed and then screamed, her tight inner muscles massaging his erection in a mind-blowing manner. Holding completely still was torture, but he wanted another orgasm from her before he let go.

Her pussy finally relaxed around him, and he pulled out almost all the way, only to slam back in. She arched as much as she could, her desperate cry galvanizing him. He continued to play with her, coaxing her little clit back to hardness, driving her ruthlessly toward her peek again. She tightened around him, and he had to fight to move again, loving the drag of her flesh gripping him.

"Mmm, *aquí mero*, right there. *Más recio, ay, me vas hacer venir.*" She arched and rocked with his strokes. "Isaac, oh, Isaac."

The tenderness in her voice affected him more than her passionate cries, and he pinched her nub between his fingers, gently rolling it back and forth. She screamed and bucked against him as her orgasm triggered his own. With a bellow he slammed into her as far as he could go and let her pussy suck the cum out of him. It felt so fucking good. He couldn't remember anything ever feeling better than emptying himself in Lucia. Even as his body poured into hers, his heart filled with her, drinking in her beauty, her kindness, and her passion.

All for him. Only him.

With a groan he pulled out and collapsed next to her, sweat cooling on his skin. For a long time neither of them moved, and as reality crept back in, he wanted to kick himself in the ass for having had sex with her. He'd broken his own rule for her, and he didn't like how much power that gave her over him. Already he knew one taste would not be enough, but he couldn't be what she needed or what she deserved. He was broken inside and had been for so long he didn't think anyone or anything could fix it.

Disgusted with himself, he pushed off the bed and avoided her gaze when she rolled over to look at him. He pulled a pair of his pants off the back of the chair near the window and jerked them on, avoiding her questioning gaze the whole time.

"I'll be downstairs. You can use the shower first."

Out of the corner of his eye, he caught her frown. "Why don't we shower together?"

He walked toward the door, unable to shake the feeling he was running from her. "No, I've got to check in with my business and make some calls."

"Okay."

The hurt in her voice stabbed at him, making him feel like the biggest asshole on earth. He wanted to turn around, to go back in there and carry her into the shower, to take care of her forever. That thought made his heart slam against his ribs, and he rubbed his chest.

"Isaac?"

He paused at the top of the stairs and turned around, looking over her shoulder and trying not to notice how well fucked she looked. "Yes?"

"Was it really that bad?"

His jaw fell, and he closed it with a snap. "What?"

She laced her hands together in front of her but squared her shoulders. "That, us, in there. Did I disappoint you?" Her voice choked on the last word.

Before he knew it he'd crossed the short distance between them and had her in his arms, cuddled to his chest.

She tried to push him away, but he held her closer. "Lucia, you deserve better. I can never be the kind of man you need. What happened in there was a mistake."

Her growl in response should have warned him, but when she stepped back and preformed a perfectly executed leg sweep on him, laying him out flat on his back, he couldn't believe that his sweet little Lucia had done that. Oh, but she didn't look sweet now. She looked pissed.

Really pissed.

His suicidal libido stirred and suggested he pull her down here with him, but he didn't want to lose any limbs. "What was that for?"

She stood over his legs with her feet spread, giving him a glimpse of her still-wet sex. A primal part of him roared in satisfaction that some of that moisture was caused by him coming inside her.

"I don't want better. I want you."

His chest tightened, and he vaguely wondered if he was having a heart attack. There couldn't be any other explanation for the sudden thudding of his heart and this dizzy feeling. Doubt and hope clashed within him, making him feel unbalanced, exposed. He hated being so vulnerable to a woman, opening himself for the emotional pain of her eventual betrayal. He wanted to believe Lucia would never do that to him, but he couldn't be sure and loving her was just too big of a risk. God, he wanted to trust her, but he just couldn't. His ex-wife had eviscerated that part of his soul.

"No, you don't."

She sat down on his chest with a thump and leaned down until their noses almost touched. She was so fucking sexy when she was pissed. "Yes, I do. Now the question is, why don't you want me?" A touch of pain raced across her dark eyes, and he felt like a complete dick.

"Lucia, I do want you."

The sincerity of his words seemed to reach her, and she momentarily cupped his face with one hand. "Well, then, why don't you take me?"

Struggling against himself he gave her a cold smile. "I thought I just did."

She growled again, but before she could attack him, he flipped her over and pinned her to the soft carpet of his hallway with his body. "Look, Lucia, I'm fucked up, okay? I don't know if I'll ever trust a woman enough to give myself to her."

In response she buried her hands in his hair and pulled him down for a hard, angry kiss. Their mouths slanted together, each desperate for the other. This felt so right, so good.

She broke their kiss by biting his lip and glared at him when he pulled back. "I never pegged you for a quitter."

Shocked, he pushed off her and sat back on his heels. "You have no idea what you're talking about."

She stood and wiped her mouth. "You're right, I don't know what happened with you, but guess what? Bad relationships happen to everyone! I can't count how many times I've been in a shitty relationship and had my heart broken, but I don't give up." She closed her eyes and took a deep breath. "Do you really want to spend the rest of your life alone in this big apartment, rattling around like the last pea in a tin can? Are you really happy like this?"

He looked away and stood up, brushing imaginary lint from his pants. "Yes."

Liar, liar, liar.

She shook her head. "I don't understand. Why would you want to be alone?"

"I've had enough of this conversation." He walked past her, keeping a wide berth in case she decided to launch an attack at him again. Who knew his Kitten had moves like a ninja? With his heart in his throat, he paused and kept his face to the wall as he said, "I'll let you know if I get any updates about the blackmailer. You have use of my entire apartment. If you're hungry, please feel free to use the kitchen or order yourself something from room service."

She didn't reply, and he took long strides down the hallway, trying to tell himself he wasn't running away from her.

Chapter Thirteen

Lucia grabbed her cell phone, her throat already closing up as she flopped back onto her exquisitely comfortable bed in the guest room. Unlike Isaac's bed, these sheets didn't smell like him. She turned her phone on and scrolled through her list of messages. An unfamiliar number came up, and she frowned. She selected that message and brought the phone to her ear.

"Hi, Lucia, this is Laurel. I just wanted to let you know I'll need you to stop by the shop to look over your costume for the Valentine's Day party. I think I've got what you wanted, but I want to make doubly sure before I do the finishing touches."

Her phone beeped, and she ended the call, staring up at the ceiling. Isaac's flip-flopping moods were giving her emotional whiplash, and she didn't know what to do. What could have happened that was so horrible?

Her eyes widened, and she picked up her phone again. She didn't know what happened, but Laurel might.

On the second ring the other woman picked up. "Hi, Lucia."

She had to clear her throat before she could speak, Isaac's rejection starting to sink in as her anger faded. "Hi, Laurel. Can I ask you a question?"

"Sure, kiddo. What's up?"

"What happened to Isaac to make him swear off relationships forever?"

Laurel blew out a long breath. "Well, that's not quite what I was expecting. Why do you ask?"

Her anger resurfaced. "Because one minute he acts like he love—er, likes me, and the next he's as cold and distant as can be." She groaned and rubbed her palm against her forehead. "I don't know if I can deal with this. He really hurt my feelings this morning."

"This morning?"

She quickly explained the situation to Laurel, leaving out the part about having sex. The other woman was quiet for a moment. "I'm coming to pick you up."

"What?"

"Just take a shower and make sure you're all buffed, shaved, and ready to go."

"I wax," she muttered as she sat up. "Laurel, I can't leave."

"Yes, you can, and you will. Look, I love Isaac dearly, but he needs a good kick in the ass. I have an idea that might do the trick."

Lucia tiptoed to the elevator and prayed Isaac didn't hear the chime of the doors opening. Unfortunately fate was conspiring against her, because the moment the doors started to slide open, he came into the foyer, now fully dressed in a suit and dark green tie, looking better than he had any right to.

His gaze narrowed, but his distant expression stayed in place. "Where are you going?"

Her heart pounded hard enough to add a slight tremble to her voice. "That's none of your concern."

The doors to the elevator started to close, but she jammed a hand in to keep them open. If they closed, he'd have more time to talk to her and might even manage to convince her to stay. But nothing between them would change, and she'd only be setting herself up for even more heartbreak.

Hurt flashed across his face before he once again schooled his features into his usual arrogant look. "Lucia, be reasonable—"

If she hadn't been keeping her hand in the door, she would have been tempted to choke him. "Reasonable? Oh yes, let's talk about reasonable. You have not only fucked me, but you fucked me over."

He didn't say anything, just crossed his arms and stared at her.

"What? Nothing to say? Yeah, I thought so, because you know that you're a fucking asshole." She stepped into the elevator, and he made a move to come after her. "You can't keep me here, Isaac. I don't belong to you, and I never will. Thank you for showing me your true colors."

Still he said nothing, but his whole body radiated tension. He opened his mouth to say something, then shut it again.

The doors started to slide closed, but she put her hand out one more time to stop them. "Oh, and you're no longer my business partner. I know enough to throw the party, and I want you to stay far away from me. I'd say our relationship is over, but we never had one. All I was to you was a means to an end, a convenient hole to fuck, and I understand that now."

"Lucia, wait—"

The pain in his eyes almost stopped her, almost made her go to him, but her rage still burned bright. She remove her hand from the elevator door and stared at him as the doors slid shut, a small part of her wishing he'd taken two steps forward to stop her, but in the end, he did nothing, and that hurt worst of all.

The sounds of the hotel lobby washed over her as the doors to her elevator opened. A woman behind the desk next to the row of elevators smiled at her, and Lucia smiled back, a blush burning her cheeks. There was no way the hotel employee could have known what she'd been doing upstairs, but she still felt like she was doing the walk of shame as she made her way to the front of the room.

Laurel spotted her first. "Lucia, over here." The tall redhead wore an impeccably tailored mint-green dress that flattered her angular frame.

"Hi, thanks for coming."

"You're most welcome, sweetheart." She pursed her lips and looked closer. "Have you been crying?"

"No, not at all."

Renewed tears burned in her eyes, and Laurel sighed. "Come on. You can tell me in the car."

They silently walked out the front door together, and Lucia turned her face up to the cold winter sun. She'd brought her purse along with her but had left the rest of her stuff at Isaac's. Later tonight, if things didn't improve, she was going to her parents' house. There was no way anyone could get near her there with her family surrounding her. Then again she really didn't want to bring all this drama home with her. Maybe she'd find a cheaper hotel to stay in. God knew she couldn't afford more than one night here at the Excalibur.

Laurel hit her car alarm, and a big black SUV beeped. "Here we go. I've got the seats warming up for us."

The warmth of the leather embraced Lucia as she got in, and she pressed her chilled hands beneath her butt. "So, I, um, I bet you're wondering what is going on."

Laurel turned on the car and pulled carefully out of

her space. "Let me guess. Isaac's fear of commitment has overruled every brain cell he has, and he's trying to push you away."

"How did you know?"

"Honey, I've known Isaac since before he got divorced. His family and my family go way back. You know, incestuous upper-crust breeding and all of that." Her lips thinned, and she stared out the windshield. "I've always hated the way he goes through women, but until you, I don't think he ever really cared about any of them."

"He cares about me? I highly doubt that."

"Of course he does. I've seen the way he watches you, and when he talks about you, his whole face lights up. He really likes you, and it probably scares him to death. Men are such fragile creatures about their emotions."

"Somehow I'm really having a hard time dredging up any sympathy for him."

"I don't blame you in the least. He acted in a deplorable manner, but he has his reasons for being the way he is."

"Can we just not talk about him right now?"

"Of course."

Lucia's anger began to fade, but the hurt remained, mixed with some guilt for lashing out at Laurel. Soon curiosity began to nibble at her resolve to not talk about him. What possible reason could Isaac have for being such a complete douche bag? They rode in silence until Lucia couldn't stand it anymore.

"I'm sorry for snapping at you, Laurel. Can you please tell me what happened to make him so cold?"

Laurel nodded. "No offense taken. It's not a big secret or anything. It couldn't be, not after it was splashed all over the gossip pages. Do you remember what your first love was like as a teenager? How utterly stupid you got over him and how you thought he hung the sun, moon, and stars?"

An unwilling smile tugged at her lips, and she leaned back into her seat. "Billy Higgins. He played for my high school football team, and I was a cheerleader. We broke up not long after prom when I wouldn't put out."

"Isaac married his first love, and she was a total and utter skank."

Lucia raised her eyebrows at the venom in Laurel's voice. "What did she do?"

"You have to remember he was only eighteen at the time, a far cry from the man he is now. She played all kinds of mind games with him, cheated on him, and distanced him from all his family and friends. This continued for about a year before Isaac's parents got sick of it and froze all of his bank accounts."

"Wow, they really didn't like her."

Laurel gave a dry laugh. "She tried to seduce Isaac's father."

"No fucking way!"

"Oh yes fucking way. Even worse, when Isaac's father told him, Isaac accused his father of trying to take advantage of Elena."

"Elena, that's her name?"

"Yep. Anyways, Elena had Isaac totally wrapped around her finger, but when Mommy and Daddy cut the funding for her high-spending partying ways, she divorced Isaac and took half his money without batting a false eyelash."

"Wow, that's really messed up."

"Yep. Isaac was crushed, and it took him years to finally trust a woman enough to even be with her. Even then it was only submissives he could control and distance himself from." She gave Lucia a sad smile. "He only dates them long enough to release his physical urges before moving on to the next woman."

A little ember of jealousy burned in her stomach. "How many women has he been with?"

"A lot."

"Like I better run out and get tested a lot?"

"You had sex with him?"

"Um, yeah."

Laurel concentrated on the road and tapped her finger against the steering wheel. "I'm sure he has always been more than careful, and all of the women he's had have been submissives from Wicked, so it's relatively safe to assume he is clean."

"Great." She groaned and thumped her head against the seat. "The one time in my life I don't insist a guy use a condom, and he turns out to be a man whore."

Laurel laughed. "Well, I wouldn't go that far." She glanced over at Lucia, then back at the road. "You have to keep in mind that up until his divorce, Isaac had a rather sheltered life. He went to an all-boys school, and his parents pretty much spoiled him. I guess the best way to put it is he'd never had to face adversity before, so he was more unprepared than most to deal with the heartache and betrayal."

"Hmm, that makes sense. I mean, I'd had a couple of boyfriends before I met Billy, so I had already been through the great and dramatic teenage breakup."

"Right, you had some coping mechanisms. Isaac, having grown up in a gilded cage, had pretty much none, and he didn't know how to handle it."

"It's hard to imagine him ever being young and insecure."

"Did Isaac tell you I invited you and him to my party tonight? It's a private party for our BDSM friends. I thought it would give you an idea of how some members of Wicked play in a more intimate setting."

Confused by the sudden change in subject, she shook her head. "No, he didn't mention anything about it."

"I figured as much. I think he needs a little shake-up, something to make him realize how much he cares about you. Feel like causing a bit of trouble?"

"As long as I don't end up in jail, sure."

"That's my girl. Let's grab some lunch and head to my salon for some pampering, my treat."

"Oh no, I couldn't let you—"

"Don't worry, if it bothers you that much, I'll have Isaac pay me back." She winked. "Come on. A little facial, some soaking in the herbal baths, maybe a massage."

Lucia rubbed the back of her neck. "I am a little sore..."

"That's my girl. If Isaac turns out to be a total dipshit, there are some very eligible Doms who will be at my party who would fight each other to the death for the pleasure of your company."

"Gladiator style?"

"Ooh, good idea. We can oil them down and let 'em go at it."

Both women laughed, and Lucia looked out the window, wondering if once again she'd be the one who ended up with a broken heart.

As Lucia gazed around Laurel's closet, she wondered if having a two-story shoe rack with a sliding ladder was normal among the superrich. It reminded her of vast library bookshelves, but instead of tomes of knowledge, they held enough high heels and boots to dress an army. Right now she sat at Laurel's expansive vanity while the other woman put the finishing touches on her makeup. The mirror was covered with one of Laurel's robes in order to surprise Lucia.

"Now look up," Laurel said in a distracted voice.

Lucia obeyed, looking up at the floral fresco on the ceiling. The tiny brush tickled her face as Laurel traced some liquid gold eyeliner around her eyes. After they'd returned from the spa, Laurel had dragged her into the closet and made her try on a dizzying array of outfits until she found one they both liked. Laurel had poked, prodded, and lifted every part of her body, but Lucia wasn't worried the other woman was making a pass at her. If anything, Laurel seemed to view her as a big doll to play dress-up with.

"There. I think we're done. You ready for the big unveil?"

"Sure."

"Oh come on, I need more excitement than that!"

She mustered up a smile that felt more like a snarl. "Yippee."

Laurel snorted, then turned and pulled the blue silk robe off the mirror. With a soft gasp, Lucia leaned forward and stared at herself. "Holy crap."

Instead of a top she wore what looked like layers of gold chain shimmering with amethysts and emeralds to cover her breasts. They were actually sewn to an ultrafine mesh that clung to her chest like a bra in order to keep the chains in place, but there were still hints of her breasts showing through. The back was completely open, and a cute and flirty black skirt complemented her curves. Laurel had done her eyes in heavy kohl eyeliner, then outlined that with a thin line of gold paint. Her lips were a deep and glossy mauve that went well with her skin tone. Laurel had straightened her hair until it hung in a superstraight and silky sheaf down her back.

"Seriously, you are amazing." She fingered the gold chains, turning this way and that to watch them sparkle.

Laurel held up her hand. "Oh, one more thing. Well actually, two more things. I'll be right back, and don't you dare text Isaac!" The full cream silk skirt of Laurel's almost transparent dress swirled around her feet as she went off in search of some new toy to put on Lucia.

She stuck her tongue out at the other woman's retreating back and sighed at her own foolishness. Isaac had texted her phone at least a dozen times today and left her a variety of messages. Laurel forbade her from contacting him, instead calling him herself and telling him that Lucia was safe with her. While Lucia had been straightening her hair, Laurel e-mailed Isaac and let him know Lucia would be coming for her things after the party.

Thank goodness Laurel was on her side, because that woman was an expert at mind games.

"Here we are," the redhead said with a smile. In her hands she held two golden combs with scarabs on them. She slid them into Lucia's hair, holding it back from her face. "Perfect."

"Are you sure this is a good idea?"

"Absolutely. Worst-case scenario is Isaac never shows up, and you play with one of the yummy single Doms instead. Once you see these guys, you're going to drool just like the rest of us."

She didn't think anyone would attract her the way Isaac did, but she didn't want to sound any more pathetic to Laurel than she already did. "I feel like I'm going to throw up."

"Nerves?"

"Yeah. I've never been to anything like this before."

Laurel laughed and sat next to her on the wide blue velvet bench. "First, let me assure you it won't be like a scene out of a porno. There will be playing, but if you stay by the pool, things shouldn't get too crazy out there. If you find someone you want to play with, head for the game room, but check with me first. I'll tell you if he is a good choice." She bit her lower lip. "Okay, so there might be some play going on by the pool, but if you're uncomfortable with it, please feel free to leave at any time. Most of our friends aren't exhibitionists—powerful men tend to not want to share their toys—but there will be a few couples there that like to put on a show."

"Okay." Her voice came out in a high-pitched squeak.

With a laugh Laurel gave her a one-armed hug. "You should see how wide your eyes are. That innocence is going to attract the Doms like nothing else. But remember, no one is allowed to do anything to or with you without your consent. If you yell the word 'red,' we'll all come running.

"Okay. Stand up." Laurel handed her two gold chains festooned with tiny bells. They made a light tinkling ring when Laurel shook them. "These are anklets. Put one on either leg."

Lucia did, then giggled when she walked across the room. "I sound like a Christmas sleigh."

"You look amazing. Ready to go break some hearts?"

"Yep," she said and took a deep breath. Aside from the Isaac drama, this party offered her a chance to rub elbows with some of Washington's elite, and she wasn't about to pass up that chance. If she had to put up with some naked people doing God knows what, so be it. A little voice in her head whispered she might enjoy watching other couples, but she quickly squashed it.

Laurel led her through the enormous Mediterranean-style house to the pool room. She'd been expecting some type of indoor swimming pool with maybe chairs scattered about but nothing like this. First off, it was huge. A giant circular in-ground pool dominated the center of the room. At the far end of the pool, it turned into a rough rock wall that somehow looked natural. There was an alcove in the rock wall, and a lovely bronze mermaid relaxed on the rocks, one hand lifting her hair off her neck. Water rushed over the rock she sat on and fell into the pool below with a gentle splash.

Men and women in various states of dress milled around the pool on pale wood floors, and elaborate windows looked out into a garden where tasteful spotlights illuminated various trees and flowers. Wrought-iron circular tables were arranged around the perimeter of the pool. Toward the back was a group of overstuffed chairs and couches arranged like a seating area. Lucia let her gaze wander back to the crowd and was relieved to see that only a few women were topless, and nearly all the men were clothed. A few men sat at women's feet in either faded jeans, leather pants, or a kilt.

"Wow."

A tall man with graying hair and sharp features hailed Laurel from across the room. "Hey, you hot redhead. Come here."

Laurel grinned and flipped her hair over her shoulder. "That's my husband, Kyle. I'd better go see what he wants before he takes a paddle to my ass."

Lucia tried to keep her tone light and confident. Unfortunately her voice came out in a squeak as she said, "Okay. I'll hang out here."

"See those two Doms seated in the far left corner? The guy with the beard and the guy with the long hair? They are all friends of Isaac. They know what's going on. Head on over there, and they'll take care of you."

With that Laurel left Lucia standing awkwardly in the doorway. Gosh, this felt like the first day of school in a weird way. She took a deep breath and stepped farther into the room, trying to take it all in without staring. Easier said than done, especially when she noticed a young woman vigorously giving her Dom a blowjob to her left.

A male voice came from directly behind her. "Hey, I didn't expect to see you here."

She turned around and looked at a vaguely familiar and cute young man with dark black hair and a pierced lip. Dressed in a pair of tight leather pants, he had a series of straight red welts across his stomach. "I'm sorry. Do I know you?"

He gave her a coquettish look from beneath his lashes. "You were bartending the other night at Wicked, and I mistook you for a Domme."

She smiled, relieved that he wasn't someone she knew out in the real world. "Oh, of course. How could I forget you in those leather pants?"

"My Mistress likes them as well."

"I'm sure she does."

He gave her a look that for some reason set her on edge before saying, "Do you want to come play with me? I can show you some tricks to being a sub. If I'm not mistaken, you're pretty new at this."

"Umm, no thanks." He frowned, and she hurriedly added, "I'm expected by some Doms." She pointed to the corner where two men sat, observing them.

"Yeah, you don't want to keep Master Hawk and Master Jesse waiting." He tilted his head to the side. "I thought you were with Master Isaac."

Hurt sliced through her chest, but she managed to keep smiling. "Oh, we're more business partners than anything else."

His jaw tensed, and his shoulders stiffened. "Well, I better get going. See you around."

She waved at his retreating back and wondered what she'd done to offend him. Then again, he could be reacting to someone or something else going on around them. He reached the far side of the room and knelt next to an extremely pale woman with jet-black hair in a black latex dress. She absently patted his head while continuing to chat with another Domme.

A brisk slap followed by a cry had her spinning on her heel, instinctively seeking out the source of the sound. To her embarrassment she got an eyeful of a woman's jiggling buttocks as her Dom bent her over his lap for a spanking. Memories of Isaac's touch flared through her, and she turned away, keeping her gaze on the ground until she reached the couches where Isaac's friends sat.

To her relief they were alone and drinking beers, with a third unopened beer on the driftwood and glass table in front of them. They both looked at her with such intensity that she almost bolted. If she ran now, she wouldn't stop running until she got back to her safe, boring little world back at her apartment. Plus, she hadn't come this far to be scared away by two incredibly handsome men giving her a thorough visual appraisal.

The man on the dark suede couch was the same man she'd seen at Wicked. His long black hair was held back in a tight braid, and he wore skintight black leather pants and a black T-shirt that clung to his lean and muscled frame. Yummy. He raised an eyebrow, and she flushed, realizing that she was staring.

Switching her gaze to the other man, she smiled in relief as she realized he was the big Texan she'd met at Wicked. He smiled back, and his bright blue eyes gleamed with mischief. Dressed in a pair of well-used jeans and a brown leather vest with no shirt beneath, he certainly was nice to look at.

She gave them a little wave and shifted from one foot to the other. "Hi, um, I'm Luc—er, Kitten." Heat blasted up her chest and to her scalp at how silly it sounded to call herself that.

Hawk spoke first, his voice low and mellow. "So this is the little woman who's been driving Isaac insane."

The Texan tipped his bottle in her direction. "Have a seat, Kitten. In case you forgot, my name is Jesse."

She took a seat on the opposite end of the couch from Jesse, intimidated by Hawk's stern expression. "Nice to meet you."

Jesse smiled and set his beer on the table before grabbing the unopened one and twisted off the top before handing it to her. "Here, you look like you could use a drink."

Gratefully she took a sip and relaxed a little bit. "Thanks. It's been a heck of a day."

Hawk grunted. "So we heard."

Anger kindled in her belly as she thought about everyone knowing her and Isaac's personal business. "What exactly did you hear?"

"That Isaac has feelings for you, but he's too chicken shit to act on them."

"He is not chicken shit!"

Jesse laughed, and Hawk's lips turned up in the barest of smiles. "Glad to hear you think that. He needs a woman who believes in him."

Jesse propped the edge of his boot on the table, creating a distracting sight with his jeans clinging to his muscled thigh. "Did Laurel fill you in on our plan?"

She shook her head and promised herself later she would have a little talk with Laurel about springing shit like this on her. "No. What plan?"

"Well, I talked to Isaac about an hour ago and mentioned you were here looking hotter than a June bride riding bareback in the moonlight."

She giggled, unable to resist his playful charm. "That hot, huh? But why did you tell him that when you hadn't even seen me yet?"

"Because no man on earth who cares about a woman wants her to be somewhere like this without him. Add to that Isaac's possessive streak, and you have a man that is hauling ass right now to come here and claim you as his."

She slumped back against the couch. "I don't know if I really want to be with a guy who only wants me like a toy that he has to keep away from others."

Hawk's deep voice stroked along her skin like velvet. "Isaac has never given a shit before if anyone wanted the sub he was currently playing with."

"Yep, he usually dumps them and lets the other Doms try to win them over." Jesse caught her bewildered look and shrugged. "He's not a complete ass. If he sees that his sub of the moment might have a chance at a real relationship with someone else, he releases her."

"But with you"—Jesse laughed and rubbed his lips—"with you he threatened to cut my dick off and feed it to the goats if I let anyone get near you before he gets here."

His words both warmed and irritated her. "I'm a big girl. I can decide who I do and don't want to talk to. Besides, he said this morning that there wasn't going to ever be anything between us."

Both men laughed, and Jesse leaned over to pat her knee. "Honey, when I talked to him a couple of days ago, he was practically writing sonnets in your name."

She tried to keep from looking too hopeful. "Really?"

"Yep. He kept going on and on about how smart you were, how brave, how beautiful, blah blah blah."

The knowledge that he was bragging to his friends about her helped thaw the chunk of ice she'd been carrying around in her stomach since this morning. "Why are you helping me?"

Hawk leaned forward. "Because he is our friend, and he's been hurting and lonely for a very long time."

"Besides, if you and Isaac don't work out, it doesn't hurt to get a little flirting time in with you. See if you want to ride a real Texas mustang." Jesse winked, and she shook her head.

"You are trouble in a ten-gallon hat."

He laughed and set his beer on the table. "Sugar, you don't know the half of it."

Hawk grunted. "Don't listen to him. He's hung more like a Texas mouse than a mustang."

She burst out laughing, and Hawk's lips turned up in his version of a smile.

Giving Hawk an affronted look, Jesse adjusted himself. "Your mom doesn't complain."

She covered her face with her hands. "Oh no, we've descended down the intellectual ladder to the depth of *yo' mama* jokes."

"Hold on, my ass is vibrating." Jesse reached into his pocket and pulled out his cell phone. "Well, speak of the devil. Excuse me for a second."

She nodded and took another sip of her beer, her nerves getting wound tighter by the minute. Her back was to the rest of the room, but she could hear the festivities heating up. The sounds of flesh being smacked, moans, and cries of passion blended in with the bubbling of the fountain. Her imagination ran wild with all the things that could be happening, and heat swept through her lower half as she imagined doing those things with Isaac.

"Hey, Isaac, what's up?" Jesse grinned and pulled the phone away from his ear, putting it on speakerphone so they could all hear.

Isaac's voice blasted through the speakers. "Where is

she?"

"Whoa, easy there. You almost busted my eardrum. Should you be talking on your phone and driving at the same time?"

"Fuck you. I'm pulling up Laurel's street now. Where is she?"

"She who?"

She had to stifle a giggle at Jesse's teasing expression, and even Hawk cracked a grin.

Isaac's voice came out in a deadly growl. "Lucia. Where is she? I told you to keep an eye on her until I got there."

"Oh, she's okay. She's with Hawk right now in the spider room."

"What? You rat bastard son of a bitch. You said you would watch over her for me until I got there! I swear if anything happens to her, I'm going to—"

"Jeez, what's the big deal? Laurel said Lucia—sorry, I mean Kitten—was here to learn about the lifestyle. It's not like you give a shit about who your subs play with after you're done with them."

"If he lays one motherfucking finger on her, I'm going to kill him!"

"She sure is a sweet little armful, all curves and spice. Does she purr when she comes?"

Isaac let loose a stream of profanity that was almost poetic in its imaginative use of swear words, threats, and body parts.

"What? I can't hear you, man. You're breaking up."

"Jesse, you better—"

"Sorry, man. I can't hear you. Are you driving through a tunnel or something? Oh, Hawk is signaling me to come to the spider room. Looks like that sweet little Latina wants to play with two men."

"I'm going to fucking—"

Jesse hung up on him, and she gaped. "Wow, he sure sounds mad."

"Yep." Jesse grinned and stood up. "Mad like a man in love."

Hawk chuckled and stood as well, giving her an eyeful of a deliciously tight ass as he turned and stretched.

"Come on, Kitten."

She stood and tried to arrange her outfit to cover as much of her body as she could with trembling hands. "Where are we going?"

"To the spider room." He winked and tucked her arm into his. "We're going to help you spin a web to capture a reluctant Dom."

Chapter Fourteen

Isaac threw the keys to his car at the waiting valet. The rage boiling through him must have shown on his face, because the valet dropped the keys and picked them up with muttered apologies. Isaac kept walking and brushed past the pretty maid inside of the front door waiting to take guests' coats.

The sound of people having a good time grew louder, and he fought the urge to run. How fucking dare she go with Hawk and Jesse? When he found her, he was going to paddle her ass until it was as red as a stop sign or at least until she admitted that she belonged to him and only him. Just the thought of either of those men, even though they were among his closest friends, touching her drove a spike of pain through his heart.

The hallway between the pool and the playrooms was crowded with people chatting and laughing. He snarled his way through, leaving a path of protests in his wake. All day long he'd been losing his mind over Lucia being gone. The accusations that she'd hurled at him, all true, had not only enraged him but helped to crack the final wall guarding his heart.

At first he thought her family had come to pick her up, but Laurel had called him soon after to let him know Lucia was at her house. He'd demanded to talk to her, but Laurel refused, telling him he didn't deserve such a kind and wonderful woman if he was going to treat her like trash. Then she'd hung up on him.

Seemed to be a running theme in his life today.

For the rest of the day, he'd sat on his couch, staring out the window and trying to decide if he should go after her or not. On one hand, if he stayed away, they could make a clean break of things, and Lucia could be happy. On the other hand the thought of Lucia giving her love to someone else made him sick. That feeling only compounded when Jesse called him from Laurel's party and talked about seeing Lucia there looking all luscious and alone. His primal side had roared to life at that mental image, demanding he get there and show her who she belonged to, who would take care of her and see to her every need.

There was no one else in the world who could possibly care for her like he did.

The spider room sat at the back of the house in a secluded corridor dedicated to the owner's kinky side. The crowd thinned out the closer he got to the play wing. He turned a corner and paused, trying to make sense of the scene before him. A man with dark hair in a pair of black leather pants held what looked like either a phone or a digital camera in his hand, and he was trying to quietly open the door.

Isaac stepped back so the man couldn't see him if he looked down the hallway and watched the man wince when the door made a slight creak. As he looked closer at the man, he realized it was Lady Morgana's sub, and the pieces started to fall into place. Adam, submissive to the woman who used to do the parties for Wicked, and a graphic designer if Isaac remembered correctly. Someone with knowledge of photo manipulation and a bone-deep desire to please his Mistress.

Moving as silently as he could, Isaac walked up behind

Adam and wrapped his arm around the other man's throat, getting him into a submission hold. Adam gave a distorted scream and dropped his digital camera while clawing at Isaac's arm.

"What the fuck do we have here?" he asked in a deceptively mild voice. Adam made some garbled reply, but he ignored it. "I'm going to remove my arm, but if you do anything other than follow me meekly to talk with your Mistress, I'm going to press charges against you. And trust me when I say I have enough money to keep you in court for the rest of your life."

Adam bent over, gasping. "I didn't do anything."

Isaac shook his head and picked up the digital camera, easily fending off Adam's halfhearted attempt to get to it first. "Really? So what were you doing with this camera?"

The door to the spider room opened, and Jesse stepped out. His smile fell from his face as he took in the scene, and he quickly closed the door behind them. "What the hell is going on?"

Adam tried to run, but Isaac stopped him with a well-placed kick to his gut. "Adam here was trying to take pictures of you inside of the spider room. More specifically he was trying to take pictures of Lucia to use as blackmail fodder."

With a low groan Adam pushed to his feet. "Was not."

Jesse rubbed his lips. "Let me get Hawk."

He opened the door and yelled for the other man, then stepped back and shut it quickly after Hawk joined them.

The Native American man lifted one eyebrow, his version of a shocked look. "Are we playing beat-the-sub?"

Isaac took a deep breath, his earlier anger subdued by the physical outlet of the fight. "Do me a favor. Take this piece of shit to Morgana. See if she can get the truth out of him."

Adam's eyes went wide with panic. "Please! No, don't do that! I did it, okay?"

Taking a deep breath, Isaac prayed for the patience to not pound the asshole's face into the ground. "Why?"

"You fuckwads made her so sad when you fired her." He sneered, his lips drawing from his teeth in an ugly snarl. "She loved doing parties for the club and put all of her heart and soul into them. But that wasn't good enough for you. No, you had to run out and get some spic bitch—"

Without even taking a breath, Isaac slammed his fist into Adam's chin, and the other man crumbled to the floor. Hawk and Jesse stepped back and looked down in disgust.

Isaac met Jesse's and Hawk's eyes and said in a low voice, "Tie his ass up, then get Morgana, Laurel, and Kyle. I don't want to ever see him in Wicked again."

Jesse nodded, and Hawk helped him lift the unconscious man by his armpits. "Lucia is inside, waiting for you. We never touched her."

He couldn't understand how someone could be around Lucia and not want to touch her. "Why?"

"Because, you dumb fuck, she doesn't want us. She wants you."

Hawk shook his head in disgust, and the men dragged a still-limp Adam down the hallway, leaving Isaac in a roaring silence.

He crouched down and ran his hands through his hair, trying to get the adrenaline out of his system. On the other side of that door waited Lucia, and despite what Jesse said, he felt like she was slipping through his fingers. For too long he'd let his fear of being hurt rule his life, and that needed to change.

The thought that had him opening the door wasn't about himself but about Lucia. She must be scared and wondering what was going on, and he couldn't bear for her to have a moment of fear, especially if he was the one causing it. He stepped into the room and turned to close the door behind him, giving himself a few more moments to get his shit together.

When he turned around, his jaw hit the ground, and blood rushed in a ball-tightening flood to his cock.

The room was painted a pearlescent smoky black, and far above a slowly shifting series of lights dimly illuminated different sections of the walls. At the back of the space stood an enormous stainless-steel spider web, and held to that web by Velcro straps around her wrists and ankles was Lucia.

She glared at him, and he tried not to laugh as he saw Jesse and Hawk had not only bound her to the spider web frame but had also gagged her with a leather strap fastened behind her head. He'd have to remember to get them a fruit basket or something as thanks. Now she had no choice but to listen to him, and he only hoped he could find the right words to say.

Her dark eyes grew wide as he slowly approached her, admiring the mound of jeweled chains that hid her breasts and the oh so brief skirt that exposed a delicious amount of skin.

"Lucia," he said in a soft voice and tried to hide his smile at her growling response. "I'm here to apologize."

He didn't know what she said behind her gag, but judging by the middle fingers she was currently using to flip him off, it wasn't complimentary. Her scent filled his nose as he stepped close enough to feel the heat of her body. She tried to pull away as he leaned in to her but stilled when he kissed a trail along her neck, pausing to suck on her rapidly beating pulse, and up to her ear.

The temptation to drive her out of her mind with pleasure was strong, but he owed her more than that. It became surprisingly hard to get the words out, and when he did whisper them into her ear, his voice was rough. "I'm sorry I didn't recognize you for the treasure that you are, that I hurt you out of my own selfish need to protect my heart. Truth is, Lucia, that no matter how much I tried to tell myself it was just business, you are so much more."

She made some garbled reply, and he was pretty sure he heard an "asshole" or two in there.

"Yes, you're right, I am an asshole. I should be whipped for what I said to you at my house." She grunted in agreement, and he smiled against her skin. "Please believe me when I say it is harder for me to have to open myself up to you like this than to take a beating."

He nuzzled the soft skin behind her ear and inhaled her scent again. Her hips shifted against his, and he moved so his front pressed her into the frame, enough to make her feel him but not enough to hurt. Her breasts pushed into his chest with each rapid breath, and he looked into her eyes, willing her to see his sincerity.

"In these last few days, you managed to demolish every wall I put up around myself, knock down every one of my defenses, and take over my heart before I even knew it. When you left today, a part of me died. I care deeply about you, Lucia." He leaned his forehead against hers and took a deep breath. "If you could please forgive me for being such a giant asshole, I'd like to take you out on a date."

She mumbled something and gave him pleading eyes.

"If I ungag you, do you promise not to bite me?"

Her gaze darkened, and he fought a grin. Telling her he found her fucking hot when she was angry probably wasn't the best move. He stepped away, and she made a noise of protest.

"I'm not leaving. I have to get a couple things."

Moving quickly across the room, he reached the unit of drawers and cupboards that seamlessly blended into one wall. He opened the door and angled his body so she couldn't see what he was doing. After putting a few items into his pockets, he strolled across the room to her, holding a small black towel in his hand.

She gave him a weary look but bent her head forward so he could unhook the gag. As soon as it was loose, he put the towel beneath her chin and wiped her mouth, making sure to get any excess saliva caused by the gag.

As soon as he removed the towel, she said in a husky voice, "This doesn't count as a date."

He laughed and wrapped his arms around her, kissing her head. "No, this doesn't count as a date. I was hoping you would let me make up for my earlier boorish behavior."

She rubbed her cheek against his chest. "Depends on what you have in mind."

"How does multiple orgasms sound?"

He looked down at her and saw her fighting a grin. "Well, it's not flowers, but I guess it'll have to do."

Cupping her face in his hands, he placed a gentle kiss against her lips, so thankful for the chance to do this again. "Tell me what your favorite flower is, and I'll have an acre of them planted for you."

"Honeysuckles." She sighed and searched his face. "Do you mean it?"

"Of course, you say the word, and I'll have my secretary arrange it."

"Not the flowers. I mean the part about caring for me." She flushed but met his gaze. "I can't take being rejected every time you feel insecure."

Guilt churned his stomach, but he pushed it away. "No, I won't do that to you again."

"Promise?"

"I promise."

She jerked at the bindings holding her arms to the frame. "Think you can take me down from this thing?"

He stepped back and let the desire to dominate that was always so close to the surface rise in him. "No, not yet."

Before she could protest he knelt before her and began to slowly kiss his way up her leg, pausing to nibble on her sensitive skin. Her rough moan inflamed his own passion, and he growled when the edge of her skirt brushed his head. "There is one thing."

"What's that?"

Her breath came out in a gasp as he nuzzled the soft apex between her thighs, running his nose along the silk of her panties. "I'm still a dominant man by nature, so you'll have to forgive me if I get a bit possessive of you."

Whatever her answer might have been turned into a moan as he slipped his finger under the side of her panties and ever so slowly massaged her clit with a light touch. Her back arched, and she groaned. Already slick with arousal, she soon soaked her panties with her honey.

He placed tiny stinging bites along her thigh as he continued to massage her aroused bud, drawing more blood to that area and increasing her craving for his touch.

"Oh, Isaac. Please, I need to touch you."

Keeping his lust on a tight leash became increasingly difficult with each passing second. He wanted her more than he'd ever wanted anyone in his life, and that scared him. Slowly moving his way up her body with his mouth, he stood and trailed kisses over her delicate jaw. She turned to him and whimpered when his lips brushed hers.

He straddled one of her legs and slipped a finger into her hot, tight pussy. Her sweet cries stroked over his cock like a physical touch, and he groaned when she began to thrust herself onto his hand. With his thumb he massaged her clit, and she tensed. Right at the moment that her cunt gripped his fingers, he kissed her.

She came apart beneath him, thrashing and moaning as much as she could while still bound to the frame. Each quiver of her sheath tempted him to plunge into her, to ride out her orgasm, but he made himself continue to massage her with his hand, drawing her release out until she tried to pull away from him.

Reluctantly he removed his hand and held it up to her face.

"Clean me."

Her dark eyes widened, but she did as he asked, slowly licking her honey off his fingers. The sight of her mouth shiny with her juices contracted the muscles of his body, and he joined her, their tongues swirling together until he removed his hand and kissed her. Pouring all of his pent-up frustration into the kiss, he devoured her mouth, claiming her and branding her as his.

The sharp edges of her teeth sank into her lower lip, and he pulled back. "Easy, Kitten."

"Please, Isaac, I mean, Master. Please fuck me. I need to feel you inside of me."

His cock jumped at her words, but he shook his head and stepped back. "Not yet."

The frame rattled as she jerked at her bonds and glared at him. "When I get off this thing, you are going to be sorry."

"Well then, I better make sure you're too exhausted to do any violence."

He withdrew a small pair of scissors from his back pocket and twirled them on his finger.

A hint of fear moved through her beautiful brown eyes. "What are you going to do with those?"

Instead of answering he knelt before her again. "Don't

move."

He held the edge of her skirt in one hand and with the other used the scissors to cut the cloth off her. It fell off her hips and landed in a puddle of fabric at her feet, leaving her clad in a pair of silky black panties. God, she was so aroused that he could see the hard nub of her clit pressing against the superfine silk.

Using just enough pressure to make a red line, he ran the tip of the scissors up her inner thigh, leaving a trail of goose bumps in its wake. Her breathing picked up speed, and she froze. He hooked his finger into the wet silk of her panties, pulling them far enough away so he could cut a long strip out from the middle. When he placed them back, just the edges framed her beautiful, swollen pussy.

He grasped her hips and gave a long, slow lick from the base of her sex all the way to the top, lapping up all of her arousal like she was the world's most delicious treat. She bucked against his mouth, her body still sensitive from her last orgasm. He inserted two fingers into her and stroked the inner walls of her vagina, driving her hard and quick toward another orgasm.

Latching his mouth on her clit, he finger fucked her, adding another digit, then another until he stretched her with three fingers inside of her tight pussy. Her cries echoed in the bare room, and he sat back on his heels, continuing to stroke her.

"Come for me, Kitten. Let go."

Her back bowed, and she did as he commanded, thrusting her hips against his driving fingers and squeezing him with each hard contraction of her inner muscles. When he finally withdrew his hand, she shuddered and rested her head against the back of the spider web, her mouth open and her breasts jiggling with each hard breath.

"Open your eyes."

When he was sure he had her attention, he began to

take his clothes off, revealing his body to her an inch at a time. Her satisfied smile stroked his ego, but he liked how she gasped when he pulled down his boxers and tossed them into the corner with the rest of his clothes. Fisting his cock, he slowly stroked himself from base to tip.

"Do you want this, Kitten?"

"I've never wanted anyone more than I want you, Master."

The glow in his chest expanded and pushed his arousal higher. Trying to cool himself down, he unstrapped each of her ankles but left her arms still attached to the frame. She jerked at her arms, but he shook his head.

"No, I want you like this. Helpless and needy."

A flush climbed from her neck to her ears. "If I was any more needy, I'd combust."

He picked up one of her legs and put it around his hip. "Well, we can't have that."

Using his free hand he lowered himself a little bit and rubbed the tip of his prick against her soaking-wet entrance. The silken feel of her arousal anointing his cock felt like heaven on earth. Moving slowly, he began to push himself into her, fighting her body's natural reaction to clamp down on him.

When he was halfway in, he lifted her other leg and wrapped it around his waist, bracing her back against the frame. Looking down at her face, he marveled at the depth of passion he saw there mixed with a soft emotion he never thought he'd see on a woman's face.

At least not for him.

"Open your eyes, Kitten." His voice came out in an unsteady growl.

She did as he asked, and when their eyes met, an electricity jumped between them, adding urgency to his need to be fully inside of her. With a hard thrust of his hips, he buried his erection in her soft depths, drawing a sharp cry from her. She started to close her eyes, but he pinched her ass, hard.

"I said open your eyes."

Something needy and vulnerable drifted through her gaze as he began to slowly stroke in and out of her body. He loved that, the way she surrendered to his will, going against her own urges to please him. Holding her gaze, he groaned as she moved her hips against him, the grip of her legs around his waist tightening with each thrust.

"Suck my finger."

She eagerly opened for him and swirled her velvety tongue around him, sending hot sparks to the base of his spine. After it was nice and wet, he reached beneath her and pressed against the entrance to her ass. Her immediate shudder almost unmanned him. He breeched the tight ring of her anus, thrusting his finger in and out in time to his thrusts.

"Fuck, that feels so good. Someday I'm going to put my cock in that tight little ass."

She shook her head, but he smiled and pounded into her harder. "Oh yes. You belong to me, Lucia. You are mine to play with, mine to cherish, mine to fuck." He removed his finger from her bottom and pressed as close to her as he could before whispering into her ear. "And I'm yours."

Her whole body tensed against him, and he strained to keep from coming. Angling her hips to meet his pelvis, he thrust into her two more times before she screamed his name and clenched all around his cock like a fist, milking him with her orgasm. Finally able to let go, he drove into her as deep as he could, and groaned as the burning rush of his own release shot through him, filling her again and again with his seed. Pleasure sank into every cell of his body, and as he whispered her name, he experienced what had to be the longest orgasm of his life.

When his body finally stopped twitching, he placed a kiss on her damp neck and slowly withdrew. He didn't want to leave her warmth, but she'd have some sore muscles tomorrow if he didn't get her off the web soon. She made a little mewling sound of distress that tugged at his heart.

"Shh, I'll take care of you."

He grabbed the towel on the ground and quickly cleaned himself before attending to her. With gentle strokes he efficiently washed her, the scent of their release mixing together and creating a primal fragrance that he loved. It was their unique smell, a blend of their pheromones that appealed to him more than any perfume in the world.

Tossing the towel over to the side, he unstrapped her arms and held her close as her knees gave out and she slumped against him. The chains of her top pressed into his chest, and he closed his eyes, so very grateful she'd given him a second chance. She rubbed her nose back and forth in the hair on his chest, making happy noises low in her throat.

He had to steady his own legs as he moved them over to the wall, then sat down and drew her into his lap. Warm and cuddly, she squirmed against him, and his cock twitched in response.

"Unless you want to go for round two, I suggest you stop that wiggling."

She laughed against his chest. "Sorry. I just feel so good. Like I'm floating on a cotton-candy cloud of happiness."

"A cotton-candy cloud of happiness?"

She nipped his nipple, startling a yelp from him. "Don't harsh my buzz."

Laughing, he kissed her head and held her as close as he could without crushing her and floated on his own cotton-candy cloud of happiness.

Chapter Fifteen

Valentine's Day

Lucia strolled through the throng of revelers in the grand ballroom of Wicked, now transformed into a 1920s speakeasy. From behind a privacy screen, a live band played a mixture of jazz and ragtime music, and one entire wall of the ballroom had been turned into a massive bar. She'd even found an amazing antique absinthe fountain that had drawn quite a crowd.

All around her men and women laughed and smiled, their joy becoming her joy. Across from her, a submissive wailed out her release as her Dom made use of one of the spinning roulette wheels in the gaming area that had been specially modified to allow a submissive to be strapped down. There were also poker tables, dice, and even a game of dominos that had all been modified in one way or another to become sexual games of Dominance and submission. Those had been Isaac's idea, and she had to admit her Master had a very perverted and yummy imagination.

She headed toward the bar to get a drink, mindful to stay away from the section with the glory holes, and grinned from ear to ear. Everywhere she looked someone was either examining one of her decorations with delight or laughing and having a great time. Giant paper heart lanterns hung from the ceiling and gave the room a wonderful smoky feel reminiscent of oil lanterns. The great lighting certainly flattered the club members, and more than one woman had told her she wished she had this kind of lighting in her bedroom.

An older woman in an apple-green beaded dress and a silvery mask stopped next to her and smiled. "Fabulous party, darling. Do you do more traditional events as well?"

Lucia nodded and fished around in the small pocket cleverly sewn into her white silk flapper dress. She pulled out her business card and made a mental note that she needed to get more from her purse when she had a second. "Of course. If you have an event to celebrate, I'd be more than happy to talk with you further about it."

The other woman took her card and slipped it into her bodice. "Thank you." She leaned closer and whispered, "My name is Gail Wentworth, but the club members know me as Sherri."

Lucia whispered back, "Your secret is safe with me, Sherri."

With a laugh, the woman waved and merged back into the shifting crowd. Lucia glanced at the elegant and extravagant gold watch that Isaac had given her as a one-week anniversary of their first date. They'd had quite a fight about it being too much, but they'd made an agreement that if she accepted the watch, he would stick to presents that cost under a hundred dollars. In the weeks since, she'd received a teddy bear from one of those build-your-own-stuffed-animal places and a cheesy keychain that played "When You Wish Upon a Star." Oh, and every Monday morning she received a delivery of a huge bouquet of fresh honeysuckle to her office.

Speak of the devil, she caught sight of Isaac and held up her hand, waving to him. He shuffled through the increasingly crowded ballroom, that irresistible smirk of his warming her from the inside out. Tonight he wore a sharp black suit with a white silk tie. His hair was slicked back, and he'd grown a bit of stubble to lend to the gangster look he was going for. Tall, dark, and handsome, he was everything she'd ever wanted in a man and more.

When he reached her side, he grinned and grasped her around the waist, setting her on the counter of the bar. "Hey there, doll."

She giggled and looked down her nose at him. "Hey yourself. You sure look swell tonight."

He raised her hand to his mouth, rubbing her knuckles across his lips. "Everyone I've talked to is having a fantastic time. You really went above and beyond even my wildest expectations."

She beamed at him and cupped his face in her free hand. "I couldn't have done it without you."

Trying to be casual, but failing, he tilted his head. "Notice anything different?"

She examined him closely, her gaze traveling down his body until a small gleam of gold on his lapel caught her attention. It was a small pin with an elaborate *W* in the middle of an art-deco-style circle.

"You made the board!"

He grinned and hugged her close. "Thanks in no small part to you."

"Oh Isaac, that's wonderful." She looked down at the pin again and traced the *W* with the tip of her finger.

"We are quite a team, aren't we?"

"Yes, we are. I've got the looks, the brains, and the skills while you have an excessively dirty mind."

He nipped the pad of her thumb with a growl that made everything below her belly button tighten in a warm flush of desire. "I thought you liked my dirty mind."

The world around them faded into the background, becoming a meaningless blur of sound and motion. She leaned down and brushed her lips over his. "I love your dirty mind."

He grinned, then grew more serious. Moving the stool separating them out of the way, he insinuated himself between her legs and pulled her closer until her already damp sex pressed against his hard stomach. "I love everything about you."

She blinked at him, unsure if she was hearing more into his words than he was saying. "You do?"

"Oh yes. I love your creativity, your strength, and your kindness." He took a deep breath. "I guess what I'm trying to say is that I love you, Ms. Roa. In fact, I think I've loved you since the day we met."

Her throat tightened up, and she swallowed hard. "I love you too."

His wonderful, clever hands cupped her bottom, and he kissed her thoroughly, claiming her mouth and squeezing her ass hard enough to make her groan.

"Mine," he said in a husky whisper against her lips.

"Yours," she agreed and kissed him back with all the joy filling her heart.

ANN MAYBURN

Ann is Queen of the Castle to her wonderful husband and three sons in the mountains of West Virginia. In her past lives she's been an import broker, a communications specialist, a US Navy civilian contractor, a bartender/waitress, and an actor at the Michigan Renaissance Festival. She also spent a summer touring with the Grateful Dead-though she will deny to her children that it ever happened.

From a young age she's been fascinated by myths and fairytales, and the romance that often was the center of the story. As Ann grew older and her hormones kicked in, she discovered trashy romance novels. Great at first, but she soon grew tired of the endless stories with a big, wonderful, emotional buildup to really short and crappy sex. Never a big fan of purple prose (throbbing spears of fleshy pleasure and wet honey pots make her giggle), she sought out books that gave the sex scenes in the story just as much detail and plot as everything else without using cringe worthy euphemisms. This led her to the wonderful world of erotic romance, and she's never looked back.

Now Ann spends her days trying to tune out cartoons playing in the background to get into her 'sexy space' and has learned to type one handed while soothing a cranky baby.

Loose Id® Titles by Ann Mayburn

*Available in digital format at http://www.loose-id.com
or your favorite online retailer*

The Breaker's Concubine

———+———

The CLUB WICKED Series
My Wicked Valentine
My Wicked Nanny
My Wicked Trainers
My Wicked Devil

———+———

The VIRTUAL SEDUCTION Series
Sodom and the Phoenix

*In addition to digital format, the following titles
are also available in print at your favorite bookseller:*

The Breaker's Concubine

———+———

The CLUB WICKED Series
My Wicked Valentine

———•———

The VIRTUAL SEDUCTION Series
Sodom and the Phoenix

CPSIA information can be obtained at www.ICGtesting.com
Printed in the USA
LVOW07s0027031015

456801LV00001B/106/P